Images

by

Lauri Broadbent

This is a work of fiction. Names, characters, places, and incidents are either the product of the author's imagination or are used fictitiously, and any resemblance to actual persons living or dead, business establishments, events, or locales, is entirely coincidental.

Images

Cover Art by *Diana Carlile*

The Wild Rose Press, Inc.
PO Box 708
Adams Basin, NY 14410-0708
Visit us at www.thewildrosepress.com

Publishing History
First Mainstream Thriller Edition, 2019
Print ISBN 978-1-5092-2298-8
Digital ISBN 978-1-5092-2299-5

Published in the United States of America

The pain was not subsiding. *The doctor said I would know when it was time to check in. Actually, he put it quite simply...the pain would be excruciating.*

Resigning himself to another sleepless night, Michael Peterson struggled as he dragged the overstuffed chair forward, trying to position it to face the fire. He frowned, realizing just how much the last couple of months had changed him.

"There." He gave the heavy chair one last shove. A well-worn neon tennis ball rolled out from beneath the chair. Michael bent down and picked it up; smiling, he thought about Dakota, the golden retriever mix he had adopted at the pet fair. He had been the perfect pound puppy, and they had been inseparable for many years. As he held the ball tightly, a lump formed in his throat. So many losses in such a short amount of time. *I can't change anything now...even if I wanted to.* He turned and slowly set the ball down on the coffee table. For the first time he felt truly alone.

Dedication

This novel is dedicated to my loves
Kevin, Courtney, and Carli and my new son-in-law,
Seth, who loves to read.
And also in loving memory of my parents,
Sue and Phil Edgar, who always believed in me.

Acknowledgments

To Margie, because without your help this manuscript might still be sitting on my closet shelf.

To my strong circle of friends, Sue, Nora, Jenny, Jean, Roene, Cathy, Clara, Terri, and Sydney who have supported me in so many ways I can't even begin to count them. Thank you all.

And to Jami, thank you for making my manuscript a shiny penny, enough so that someone wanted to pick it up.

And a special thank you to my editor at Wild Rose Press, Ally Robertson, for her unending guidance and support. Her knowledge and input were invaluable.

"One theory about how these new behaviors become implanted into the transplant recipient along with the organ is 'cellular memory,' i.e., the notion that somehow memories are embedded in cells."

~Bruce H. Lipton, PH.D.
The Biology of Belief
Unleashing the Power of Consciousness, Matter &
Miracles

****

'Barnyard Biotech' Hatched
Byline: Amanda Covarrubias
Associated Press—March 6, 1997

"San Diego. When is a chicken not a chicken? When it sings and bobs its head like a quail, thanks to an experimental brain-cell transplant.

"The larger implications are what this will teach us about the development of brain circuits that produce behavior," (Evan) Balaban, (an experimental neurobiologist at the Neuroscience Institute of San Diego) said Wednesday. "It could eventually help people who have brain damage or mental illness or even brain diseases."

Chapter 1

The pain was not subsiding. *The doctor said I would know when it was time to check in. Actually, he put it quite simply...the pain would be excruciating.*

Resigning himself to another sleepless night, Michael Peterson struggled as he dragged the overstuffed chair forward, trying to position it to face the fire. He frowned, realizing just how much the last couple of months had changed him.

"There." He gave the heavy chair one last shove. A well-worn neon tennis ball rolled out from beneath the chair. Michael bent down and picked it up; smiling, he thought about Dakota, the golden retriever mix he had adopted at the pet fair. He had been the perfect pound puppy, and they had been inseparable for many years. As he held the ball tightly, a lump formed in his throat. So many losses in such a short amount of time. *I can't change anything now...even if I wanted to.* He turned and slowly set the ball down on the coffee table. For the first time he felt truly alone.

Taking a deep breath, he looked around the room, grabbed a couple of extra pillows and tossed them onto the chair, hoping they might make him more comfortable. But in the end, he knew it really wouldn't matter what he did.

Easing his thin frame down into the chair, he twisted and turned trying to find a comfortable spot, but even with the added padding, it was nearly impossible. Finally settling in, he focused his gaze on the flames as they cracked and danced to a rhythm all their own. Absentmindedly, he ran his finger down the left side of his nose along the almost invisible scar, the result of his first and only attempt at playing football. Michael was hoping to clear his mind and quiet his thoughts for as long as possible in an attempt to delay the inevitable.

The last couple of times he sat through these night-long vigils he wondered if he would even see the morning again, but this was the choice he had made. He couldn't bring himself to sit in a hospital room waiting for that so-called perfect opportunity.

Within minutes his eyes began pulsating. Hour by hour the waves of throbbing increased. He took a deep breath and pushed his body deeper into the chair, gradually easing his head back until it rested lightly against the top of the seat. His knuckles whitened as he gripped the arms of the chair. He squeezed his eyes shut as the onslaught of pain proceeded to pound in full force.

****

Squinting, Michael peered tentatively around the room; its brightness made it difficult for him to make out anything. As his eyes gradually adjusted, he began to recognize the familiar things around him. His skin was sticky by the drying sweat and a slight dampness clung to his dark brown hair. He had made it through, but the tightness in his stomach and the dull ache in his head still lingered. This one was different, the worst one yet. Time was running out.

He stood up and slowly maneuvered the chair back into place, then stretched to relieve his arms and back from the tight ball he had been curled in all night. He really hadn't expected the pain would be so intense. Instinctively, he knew he probably could not ride out another one alone. He hated to admit it even to himself; he was scared.

It was time to check in.

Chapter 2

Elliot Paxton rose slowly from the comforting warmth of the bed. Pulling himself up to his full height as he stretched, he moved toward the bathroom, turning to gaze at the sleeping form twisted in the soft folds of the satin sheets.

God, she is so beautiful. Quietly, he walked back to the bed and brushed a light kiss on her forehead.

"Soon my love, soon," he whispered. Once again, he found himself wishing that Catherine had already been taken care of, but that would happen soon enough. His lips curled in calculating certainty.

Minutes later, Elliot stepped briskly from the shower, feeling refreshed. He evaluated himself critically in the mirror. Lines of age were beginning to show, yet there was no question he was still in fine shape. He smiled at his image, his white teeth instantly enhanced by his perpetually tanned face. Turning away, he frowned, running his hands through his thick, graying waves.

There were times when the age difference between Stephanie and himself bothered him, but he quickly dismissed these thoughts by thinking of the passionate—almost sadistic—way they made love. *There was definitely no age difference in that department!* Amused with his own declaration he let out a short laugh, which came out more like an animal's snort.

The sound of Stephanie stirring in the next room forced Elliot's thoughts back to the present and the confrontation that would soon take place. He and Stephanie had spent too little time together and obviously, there were several issues that still needed to be addressed, but Catherine was returning home today. *It would just have to wait.* Shaking his head in disappointment, he turned toward the kitchen.

Once dressed, Elliot hastily grabbed a cup of coffee, checked his gold watch, and headed for the front door. He had just enough time to run by the office before meeting Catherine at the airport.

He stopped and lingered in the doorway. Stephanie crossed the room, her bare feet making almost no sound on the cold tile floor. Elliot wrapped his arms around her and pulled her into his embrace, giving her a searching kiss. He slipped his hand down the teasingly low opening of her black silk robe to feel the soft mounds of her milk white flesh…she stiffened. *Shit. Well, there's no time to go into it now.* His jaw tightened; he would just have to wait, and waiting wasn't one of his strong suits.

"I love you," he said passionately, hoping for the same response in return.

"Love you, too," she replied half-heartedly, quickly kissing him goodbye.

"I'll call or see you tonight, depending on what happens." He turned and walked down the path to his car parked in front of their cozy hillside apartment in Sausalito, away from prying eyes and the publicity that would surely have followed if they had stayed in the city.

Did Stephanie really love him, or were her feelings as casual as the tone of her voice? Hadn't he just proven how important she was to him? What else could she possibly need? He had no idea.

****

Closing the door, Stephanie sat down at the small kitchen table, leaned back, and lit a cigarette. She inhaled slowly, relieved things had gone well the night before.

After Elliot had fallen asleep, she got up and snuck into the living room, flashlight in hand, to find the document that secured her future. Once it was in her possession, she quietly crept into the other bedroom, which doubled as a small office, and made two copies. Stephanie stuffed one copy in a previously addressed envelope, and hid the original, beneath a pile of bills in the top desk drawer.

Making her way back into the living room, Stephanie put the second copy back in Elliot's briefcase, hoping he wouldn't discover the switch until it was too late and nothing could be done about it.

Then she headed to the front door, checking over her shoulder to make sure Elliot hadn't gotten up. She slipped outside, walked a few feet, and shoved the envelope into the community mailbox.

She returned to the apartment and slipped back into bed, struggling to remain perfectly still, certain that the sound of her beating heart would awaken him.

The phone rang jarring her into the present. "Hello? Yes, he's gone. To the airport. I agree it's useless, but as we both know, he has to try. Sure, I'll meet you there at one. Bye, love." She stubbed out her cigarette and headed for the bedroom.

****

The drive into San Francisco was always beautiful. The fog was tucked into each little valley, playing hide-and-seek with the sun. As Elliot rounded the last curve, the Golden Gate Bridge loomed in front of him. It was a breathtaking sight that usually held a certain fascination for him. But as he deftly maneuvered his silver Mercedes with confident ease onto the bridge, his mind was not on the magnificent view. It was on Catherine.

Forty-five minutes later, he pulled up in front of the impressive thirty-two story building. It made him feel good just looking at it. Then he drove around the corner and down into the company-owned parking garage, pulled into his personal parking space, and hopped out. But instead of going through the convenient private entrance, he went through the front doors. He *always* went through the front doors. He wanted to make sure everyone was aware of his importance, not simply of his existence. Elliot Paxton wanted everyone to know he was not just a name on the letterhead.

He could still picture the first day he walked through those doors so many years ago after Catherine's father offered him a job. He had worked hard at manipulating his way up through the organization, excelling beyond what Thomas could have ever imagined. Though his methods were not always ethical, Elliot became a true asset to the company, eventually taking over when her father reluctantly stepped down.

Strutting through the spacious lobby, Elliot took everything in, right down to the missing button on the guard's shirt as he passed the security booth and stepped onto the elevator.

Riding up to the top floor, he thought about his life. While his professional goals had been more than met, his personal life was in shambles. His wife was a frigid little bitch, his son a disappointment in so many ways, and as far as he was concerned, only his daughter had any potential, though their relationship was distant at best.

When the elevator door opened, Elliot stepped out and surveyed the tastefully decorated outer office. Still, he had not done too badly for himself.

"Good morning, Mr. Paxton."

"Good morning, Grace," he responded dismissively, striding past her and into his office, closing the huge ornately carved doors behind him. He went over to his desk and spotted it immediately. There it was, sticking out from the usual stack of mail placed neatly on his desk each morning.

An overwhelming sense of satisfaction swept over him as he carefully opened the envelope and read: *Time, place, target. One half paid up front. Done. The rest to be paid automatically upon completion.* Now all he had to do was sit back and watch everything fall into place.

Chapter 3

Stephanie sat rigidly with her back to the window, her long, shapely legs crossed, and her thick auburn hair glistening in the surrounding sunlight. She was dressed conservatively, not wanting to call attention to herself. She stared down at the half empty drink in front of her, unconsciously playing with the ice.

Normally the Bayside Café was one of her favorite places for lunch, but today she wished she was any place else. She had been dreading this meeting. A decision would have to be made.

Stephanie didn't love Elliot. Then why had she done what she did? She didn't have a good answer. It was merely a way to survive. Now that Catherine was back, and most likely going to divorce him, there was no more time for debate. She needed to decide just how far she was willing to go.

She understood why Elliot had gone to the airport to meet Catherine. She also knew this last pitch of his would be futile. Whether he realized it or not, Catherine was a very strong woman, and Stephanie saw so much in her to admire.

A shadow passed over the white linen table. Stephanie peeked up over her sunglasses.

"Hello." He bent over to meet her upturned lips, and then hastily slid into the chair facing her.

"Hi, honey," she said quietly.

"Why do you look like you've just lost your best friend?" He sounded annoyed by her lack of enthusiasm. "I know, you didn't think I was coming, but babe, I would never forget about you. I had a couple of important things to take care of. Sorry if I worried you."

"No, it's not that. I was just thinking. I really don't know if I can go through with it. Isn't there any other way?" Stephanie pleaded with him, hoping he had possibly changed his mind, too. "I mean…he's going through so much right now," she said lamely, trying to explain her change of heart. But one look at his face told her he hadn't and now she had made him angry.

"Wait one damn minute here. We have gone through this too many times. You know as well as I do the old guy's an ass!" His voice got louder. People began to turn and stare in their direction.

"Shhhhhh," she whispered.

"I can give you anything that bastard can…and when I'm through with him, it will be even more!" He slammed his open palms on the table, rattling the crystal glasses. Through his clenched jaw, he asked, "So, are you telling me that you love him now?"

"No," she replied quietly, embarrassed by the scene he was causing, hoping he would calm down.

"Do you love me?" The tone of his voice had softened somewhat, but the flush of his face told Stephanie another story.

"Yes."

"Well then, I guess it's all settled. You do it my way, or we're through. And you can grow old with nothing to show for it except for being the whore of the once powerful Elliot W. Paxton! Not a pretty picture, huh, sweetheart?" He cocked his head and shrugged.

Stephanie glared at him. "You know, sometimes you can be just as much of a bastard as he is, and I wonder if I really want either of you!"

"That's okay by me, baby." He moved to get up, but Stephanie desperately grabbed for his hand.

"All right, all right. I'm still in."

"Good girl. That's what I wanted to hear," he said, with smug satisfaction in his voice. "Now, let's get back to the flat and really have lunch!" He pulled her to her feet.

****

Garrett was pleased their little scheme was moving along smoothly. So far, Stephanie had played her part exactly as he had planned. He still couldn't believe Elliot had fallen for the ruse without the slightest bit of reservation. He really was the egotistical fool they had counted on.

Sitting naked at the small kitchen table, he lit a cigarette and shifted position. "Shit," he complained, as his skin didn't shift with him. He gingerly pulled his bare skin up from the chair and rubbed the back of his leg. His mood quickly darkened recalling Stephanie's reluctance to move forward. *That bitch better not be thinking of backing out now!*

After an exceptionally satisfying session of love making, Elliot made the crucial mistake of telling Stephanie about his hidden account in Andorra. It didn't take long before Stephanie shared this information with Garrett. Hearing this, Garrett had been quick to realize that Elliot wanted Stephanie so badly he would agree to do almost anything to possess her, and to Elliot possession meant marriage.

Once he had thought it through, he quickly convinced Stephanie to string Elliot along for a while, and then to marry him, with one condition: that he make her the sole beneficiary of his offshore account in Andorra. If the marriage didn't work out she would walk away with everything in the account. Elliot happily complied with all of her requests. That stupid fool never once questioned her motives. He was such an easy target.

Sitting quietly, he reviewed his plan, it was ingenious. Within a day or two a copy of the signed document would land on the desk of Franklin White, the Scottfords' attorney, fully exposing Elliot as the cheating bastard he was. Armed with the original document of Elliot's offshore accounts as security, they'd be set for life!

Taking his plan one step further, if Catherine, by some miracle, decided not to divorce Elliot, he knew they would be able to blackmail him for years. If she chose to go through with the divorce, they would demand a large sum of money up front from him to ensure their silence about the lucrative little secret he'd kept from his wife. It really didn't matter to them which way it went; either way, they were going to be rich.

The best part of the whole thing was witnessing Elliot's slow realization that he had been set up, coupled with the distinct possibility his ass could eventually end up in court. *The great Mr. Paxton was not as untouchable as he thought he was!* There was no way Elliot would risk the humiliation of all that courtroom drama and the negative publicity that would follow. No, Elliot would make every effort to keep his marriage intact, even if it meant paying them off to save face.

Garrett got up from the chair, "Shit!" Again his skin did not go with him, but that did not deter the overwhelming urge to ensure Stephanie was still on board. Walking back to the bedroom he smiled at the familiar stirring knowing he would soon be the one on board.

****

Sitting in a white sterile room, clad only in a flimsy green gown, Michael already knew the news was not good, though he noted the doctor did his best to hide how discouraged he was.

"I'm sorry. The tests indicate a rapid increase in the growth of the tumor. You need to check into the hospital immediately."

"I can't do that, Doctor. I have so many things to take care of."

"Michael," the doctor paused, "I can't honestly say I know how you feel, but the pain will only increase. The best thing at this point is hospitalization, and even then, it would be merely to make you more comfortable. But, it would also give us an edge on the timing."

"I understand how incredibly important the timing is." Michael tried to reassure the doctor that he really appreciated him wanting to make things easier. "But I can't spend my last days, however long that is, just sitting around waiting for something to happen. I do have one question, though."

"Okay, shoot."

"Will I have any idea when the end is near?"

"No, I honestly don't think you will. It could happen at any time or place and that's exactly why I want to admit you into the hospital right now. It would definitely increase the odds of making the operation successful."

"I just can't do it, Dr. Whitney."

"I understand, even if I don't agree with you," Dr. Whitney replied, clearly displeased with Michael's decision.

Michael stood up and dressed. Without speaking, Dr. Whitney placed a hand on his shoulder. Their eyes met in a silent pact that nothing more would be said. They would both hope for the best.

Michael walked to the door and opened it, then paused as if to say something. Changing his mind, he walked out.

"I'll see you soon." the doctor said quietly to himself. He stood in the doorway watching Michael make his way down the hallway and out of the office. "And hopefully it won't be too late."

Chapter 4

"Hurry up, Maxwell!" Elliot shouted at the limousine driver. He was tense, getting more and more on edge with each passing minute.

"Sorry, Mr. Paxton, but it looks as though there's been an accident up ahead."

Elliot sighed and muttered, "I can't afford to be late. It's one of her biggest peeves. One of many, I might add. Shit. If I'd taken my own car, I'd be there by now."

He leaned back in the cushioned seat and impatiently tapped his foot, vividly recalling the events that led up to the last time he'd seen his wife.

Catherine had been standing in the foyer holding a large envelope. Instinctively, he knew that whatever was in it was not good.

She opened it and slowly pulled out the contents—picture after picture of him with other women exposed in positions that instantly stained her cheeks with anger. He was caught. He knew what was coming next, as they had been through this so many times before—the angry accusations, vicious arguments, always followed by his empty promises. This was all the proof she needed that nothing had really changed, and nothing ever would.

Elliot tried to embrace her. She jumped at his unexpected touch and pushed him away, then ran up the long staircase and into the bedroom, dropping the pictures in her hasty departure.

One by one, Elliot picked them up, cringing when he saw how explicit they were. He would never be able to explain his way out of this.

He slowly made his way up the stairs and opened the bedroom door. Catherine was sitting on the bed, her body turned away from him, locked in rhythmic sobs. Sighing, his face twisted in disgust, he crossed the room and sat down on the bed, gently placing a hand on her back.

"Honey, I'm so sorry. It will never happen again…I promise."

She froze at his touch. She turned and looked at him, and though her eyes were still filled with unshed tears, Elliot was shocked by the glare of pure hatred on her face.

"I am no longer willing to play this little game with you. I'm tired of your affairs. I've known for a long time that you haven't stopped." She paused and drew in a shaky breath. "I thought it would pass. No, actually, I hoped it would pass, but it obviously hasn't, has it?" It was a statement rather than a question. The answer was evident. "And now I see, quite literally," she spat, "it never will. I told myself to wait and be patient. And I was willing to do that for our family and the business we've all worked so hard for…I so wanted to prove that my father was wrong about you, but I couldn't, so there is no reason for us to continue with this charade."

Unflinching, Catherine looked directly into his eyes, cleared her throat, and stated calmly, "I want you out of my life." Elliot tried to respond, but she cut him off. "Shut up and listen to me. I'll be leaving for a while. By the time I return, I want any loose ends you have at the office tied up and all of your belonging cleared out!"

Elliot couldn't believe what he was hearing, but he recognized she meant every word.

"I've said everything I have to say. Now, get out of my house."

"Oh, Catherine." He again tried to embrace her, but she pushed him away with a glare.

Knowing he couldn't win this one, Elliot abruptly rose from the bed and rushed into the huge walk-in closet. Enraged, he blindly reached up to the top shelf to grab a suitcase, but instead, found himself bombarded with an array of shoes.

"Damn it!" He made one more attempt to grab what he needed. He jerked a small leather overnight case off the shelf and spun around trying to avoid more falling shoes. He yanked out drawers and pulled shirts off their hangers, shoving everything he could into the small case. He took one last look around and, satisfied he had enough to last for the time being, he snatched up the suitcase, and headed out from the back of the long closet.

As he exited, he deliberately reached out and roughly grabbed an armful of delicately beaded dresses that hung neatly in a line according to their length and color. He carelessly tossed them down and walked on top of them, dragging his heels as he went. He found the sounds of beads crunching and material ripping beneath his feet very satisfying. He looked down, smiling. His rage created a twisted rainbow of colors that now lay crushed in a heap on the closet floor. Once out of the closet, he walked straight to the bedroom door without glancing at Catherine.

"I will not let you make a mockery of me or my father's memory. I'll fight you every step of the way if I have to! You will not..."

Elliot was out of the bedroom and down the stairs before she could finish. He tried to comprehend what had just happened. He couldn't believe this was all falling apart now. He had gotten way too sloppy. There had to be a way to stall the divorce. She just needed to calm down and think things through. Given a little time, he could convince her to take him back, at least temporarily, and that was all he needed.

Elliot went out the front door and into the pouring rain. He slid into his silver Mercedes, backed down the long driveway, and moved out onto the wet pavement. Gunning the engine, he headed straight for Sausalito. The car backfired, and the gear shift was sticking. "Damn," he uttered, "it's back to the shop for you."

Elliot looked down at his watch. He was sure she had landed by now. "Shit," he said under his breath. "Maxwell, how much longer?"

"We're almost there, sir."

Elliot sat back and tried to relax. They just might make it on time. And, he was confident he'd convince her to take him back, just like he always had.

Chapter 5

"Ladies and gentleman, the 'fasten your seat belt' sign has been turned on. We will soon be landing at the San Francisco International Airport. We know you have a choice when making reservations so on behalf of the flight crew and myself, thank you for choosing our airline. We hope to see you soon and have a nice day in the city by the bay."

Catherine opened her eyes and gazed out the tiny window in time to catch the city's skyline coming into view as the plane circled and descended toward the airport. She smiled. She loved San Francisco, the city where she had been born and raised.

She had spent a month in a little cottage in the South of France, deciding what she intended to do with the mess she had made of her life. The time away gave her new strength in her conviction to follow through with the divorce, even though her family would be surrounded by scandal once again. Whatever else it might create she had no idea, but she was positive she was making the right choice.

I am so glad that my father will never know that in the end he was right about you, Elliot!

Catherine felt the plane touch down.

One thing she was sure of was that Elliot would be at the airport making that last desperate attempt to get her back. She opened her purse, pulled out her compact, and checked her make-up. She quickly ran a comb through her short blonde hair. When the plane came to a complete standstill and the seatbelt sign clicked off, she stood up and automatically smoothed out the wrinkles in her blue linen suit. Catherine lifted her chin, took a deep breath, and gracefully walked off the plane into the busy terminal.

****

The sleek black limousine pulled up outside the airport just as Catherine emerged onto the sidewalk. Elliot jumped out of the car and grabbed the computer case from her hands.

"Here, let me take that for you, darling," he oozed with saccharine charm.

Catherine glanced at him, barely able to conceal her contempt. He opened the back door for her. She stepped lightly into the waiting limousine and prepared for round one, knowing this was only the beginning of many battles to come.

Elliot climbed into the seat beside her and cleared his throat. "Catherine, I love you. I don't want to lose you. I'll do anything you ask. I'll never touch another woman again. Please, Catherine. Please. Can't we try again?"

There it was, the carefully crafted remorseful husband act. She laughed. "You're disgusting. There is no reason for you to continue to beg. It won't do any good, so let's get on with it. Have you moved your things out of the office yet?"

"Why, you little bitch. No, I haven't moved my things out!" His face flushed in anger. "I'll have them out tonight! But this is not the end of it, my dear. I've invested too much of my life for the company and it won't be that easy getting rid of me!"

Catherine sat calmly as her husband continued. "I'm going to take what is rightfully mine…and if you get in my way, I will use whatever means necessary to stop you!" His threat hung in the air between them. He rolled the privacy glass down. "Max, drop me off at the office and take Mrs. Paxton home!"

"Yes, Mr. Paxton."

The ride into the city was a long and silent one, each retreating to their corner of the back seat. Once they reached the building, Elliot got out, slamming the door behind him. Catherine's face was turned from his view. As the limousine sped away, a warm tear slid down her cheek.

****

Sitting in his spacious office, Elliot downed his fourth bourbon and looked out the huge picture windows. He watched the sun slowly set behind the gray towers of concrete and steel.

"I will not let her take all this away from me. I've worked too damn hard and kissed way too many asses."

He turned back toward his desk and opened the bottom drawer, pulling out a black metal box. Unlocking it, he searched through the papers until he found exactly what he was looking for. He pulled out the envelope and began to reread its contents.

"You'll get yours, Catherine…and real soon." Over and over again, he pictured the chaotic scene in his head. It was perfect. "There's no need for me to clear out my office, because I won't be going anywhere."

Satisfied he was in control again, he slowly folded the piece of paper and put it back in the envelope. *No phone calls, no text, no emails…no way to trace.*

Tapping the envelope on his desk, he realized the letter was the very last piece to be taken care of. *And I'll get rid of this tomorrow,* he decided, returning it to the black box. He locked it and put it back into the bottom drawer. Then he picked up the phone and punched in the numbers.

Chapter 6

"Come on, let go of me. I've got to answer the phone," Stephanie squealed. He loosened his grip just enough for her to slip away and lunge for the phone.

"Hello?" she said breathlessly. "Oh, hi Elliot. No, I wasn't doing anything. Took me so long? Uhhhh, I was cooking myself something to eat." She rolled her eyes at her stupid excuse; she really didn't like to cook much and Elliot knew that. The blanketed form in the bed laughed. Stephanie quickly covered the mouthpiece with her hand and shot him a dirty look.

"What? Elliot, honestly, I think that deep down inside you already knew she wouldn't change her mind. Yes, I get why you had to try." Two warm hands caressed her back, slowly moving to her sides. One hand began to fondle a breast, lightly pinching her nipple. The other hand made its way down her flat stomach to the dark triangle between her legs. His warm breath gently encircled her ear. Stephanie shifted her position making his access easier. Her body began to respond to his touch. It was hard to concentrate on what Elliot was saying.

"Keep him on the phone for let's say at least the next...ahh, fifty-five minutes to an hour," he whispered in her ear.

Stephanie again covered the mouthpiece. "Why?" she asked, her face twisted in confusion at his strange request.

"Just do it. String him along, then get him over here and get it over with," he barked, abruptly pulling his hands away from her open invitation and jumping out of bed.

With the phone tucked between her cheek and shoulder, Stephanie signaled for him to come back. But he turned his back to her and began dressing. She admired his tall, lean body as she watched him saunter across the room.

"Huh…what? Yes, I'm still here. So, tell me again what Catherine said?"

The front door opened and closed. He left without saying a word. *That bastard, what in the hell is he doing?*

Stephanie stared at the small clock perched on the bedroom dresser. Eighteen minutes…thirty-one minutes…fifty-seven. *There, that should be good enough.*

"Okay, I think I've got it now. I'm so sorry it didn't work out the way you wanted. Anyway, I do have something I want to discuss with you. So, why don't you come over?" She asked, pushing to end the call.

"Okay, I'll see you then. Yeah, me too. Bye." She hung up and quickly straightened up the apartment. In less than an hour Elliot would be there. *God, I've got to take a shower.* Elliot would surely be able to smell the scent of recent sex on her. Hastily, she changed the sheets and slipped into the shower, hoping to be done before he arrived.

****

Elliot hung up. Something was wrong; he could

feel it. Stephanie seemed distracted, rambling on and on, asking the same questions several times. Why had she asked him to come over? They'd already made plans to get together and discuss their future if his meeting with Catherine was unsuccessful. Which, by the way, unsuccessful was definitely an understatement. The afternoon's confrontation fell more into the classification of total disaster. He knew now the relationship was irreconcilable.

Had Stephanie forgotten everything they had planned? What in the hell was going on? After Catherine's rejection, he wasn't so sure he wanted to hear what was on her mind.

All of a sudden, he laughed. *Elliot, old man, that poor excuse of a wife has got you doubting yourself. Come on. All you need is a little loving. You'll hash out all the minor details about your wonderful life together, then hop in the sack where you always do your BEST talking. She's not at all like the frigid thing you're married to. Nope, not at all.*

Elliot rose from the soft leather chair, pulling off his tie and tossing it onto the desk. He turned and picked up his coat sliding his long arms in to the sleeves. As he turned back, the picture of a smiling Catherine sitting on his desk caught his eye.

"You spoiled little bitch. This is my company and I've helped make it what it is today! You will never take it all away from me. Never!" He spoke to the frozen image. He stepped around the massive mahogany desk and crossed the room to switch off the lights. Stopping short, he turned with renewed anger and headed back to his desk. He picked up the golden framed picture of Catherine and hurled it against the wall. The delicate frame shattered, throwing shimmering splinters of glass and gold all over the thick carpet.

He laughed. The sound of his laughter rose, as he stepped directly on the smiling face of his wife. With great pleasure, he ground the heel of his shoe straight through the center. He lifted his foot, admiring the damage he had done.

"Well, Catherine, my dear, that's exactly what is going to happen to you." Elliot smiled, crossed the room again and flipped off the lights. He left his office confident that everything was going to turn out just the way he had planned.

****

The lobby was dark except for the light in the security booth. This time, Elliot headed out the side door, which led directly to the parking garage. There sat his silver Mercedes, just back from the mechanic, gleaming despite the dimness. Pleased, he hopped in.

"Well, at least someone loves me." He affectionately patted the steering wheel.

He eased the stick into first gear and smoothly guided the car out into the dark city night. He headed to the edge of the city, deciding to drive through Fisherman's Wharf, along the bay's shoreline and up on to the Golden Gate Bridge. Driving always seemed to calm Elliot. He loved the feeling of being in total control.

Making his way onto the bridge, Elliot didn't notice the fog rolling in and the cars in front of him slowing down. Cursing, he maneuvered the sleek machine into the next lane, trying to avoid getting bogged down in traffic.

Elliot didn't see that the cars in the next lane had also slowed down. Suddenly, he found himself going too fast. Frantically he tried to downshift, but the gears appeared to be stuck. Again and again he tried, but they would not budge. He tried pumping the brakes, but nothing happened.

"Oh my God. I don't believe this! Not me. Not now!" Elliot glanced in both the side and the rearview mirrors, trying to take in all the cars around him. *Could it be possible?* His car seemed to take on a life of its own. As it lurched up and over the curb, Elliot braced himself for the pop of the airbags. Smashing head-on into the concrete guard rail, the car came to an abrupt halt. The interior of the car remained silent. The steering wheel, which Elliot had so affectionately patted, had crushed the life out of him.

Chapter 7

God, I'm exhausted. Catherine picked up her soft terry robe and went into the lavish bathroom. Slipping out of her clothes, she eased her slim form into the tepid water of the waiting bath. The marble was smooth against her skin. The lavender scent from the bath crystals was comforting in their familiarity.

"What a day." She sighed. *I knew Elliot would be there, but why on earth did he have to beg? It was so degrading for both of us. This is the last thing I need in my life right now.*

With her eyes closed, Catherine reminisced about her fairytale existence, and how her father made sure she never wanted for anything. God, she missed him terribly.

She was young and naïve when she met Elliot, and for her, it was love at first sight, but not so for her parents. Fearing Catherine was too young to know what she wanted they sent her away to college and far away from Elliot.

After several months of tears and tantrums, Catherine finally agreed to go. Miserable, she worked as though she were possessed, proved to be a quick study, and graduated early. Her parents had no other choice but to reluctantly agree to Catherine's wish, which was to marry Elliot.

Thinking back, she wished she had listened to her

parents; it would have spared her so much grief.

She had just finished up with her nightly creaming routine, as she called it, when the phone rang. She ran from the bathroom, knowing the staff had already retired for the evening.

"Hello?"

"Mrs. Paxton?"

"Yes, this is she."

"Mrs. Paxton, my name is Julianne Nelson. I am one of the chief administrators here at San Francisco Memorial Hospital, and I've called to inform you that your husband, Elliot Paxton, has been in a serious car accident."

Catherine was stunned into silence.

"Mrs. Paxton? Mrs. Paxton, are you still there?"

"I'm here," she answered stiffly.

Ms. Nelson continued. "Mr. Paxton is currently in our care on life support."

There was no response.

"I know this is not the best time, and I don't know if you're aware, but…" she hesitated. "Your husband's driver's license indicates he had signed up as an organ donor, and because of the situation, I do need to secure some type of official confirmation from the family, you specifically, Mrs. Paxton, to act upon his request if necessary."

"What? Uhhh..oh, yes, that's fine."

"Thank you, Mrs. Paxton."

"I don't want to rush you; however, it is a time sensitive issue. Is it possible for you to come to the hospital?"

The other end of the line remained silent.

"Mrs. Paxton, is there anything I can do for you?"

"No…no, but thank you for calling. I'll be there as soon as possible," Catherine said mechanically as her eyes filled with tears. She placed the receiver back into the cradle and stared out into the darkness. "Oh, Elliot, I didn't want this to happen. Honestly, Elliot, not this way, never this way."

****

Michael Peterson sat slouched in a dark corner booth. On each table, randomly placed candles flickered from inside their thick glass bowls. The light they emitted only sparsely lit the small bar. The walls were streaked with grease and the red leather upholstery was cracked and rough; it pricked his skin through his cotton shirt.

He could hear the drunken voices of the men around him; the bits and pieces of their conversations brought a slight grin. Different voices always discussing the same theme…the good life. Everywhere he went, it seemed as though everyone was caught up in that illusive fantasy.

I've had the good life, and where has it gotten me? He was a professor at a well-known college, with a relatively good salary, and a feeling that he was actually making a difference in this world. He had met the woman he intended to grow old with and they had begun planning their future together. His life had fit him like a well-worn baseball glove.

He picked up his drink and downed it in one swallow. He could still feel the familiar dull pain in his head, and despite his efforts to subdue it, it was getting stronger. He leaned his head back and stared at nothing in particular.

The pain was different this time. He slipped his

hand into the pocket of his sports coat that lay on the seat beside him. He pulled out the brown plastic bottle containing his temporary relief. Popping several small white pills into his mouth, he waited for the pain to subside.

The increasing pain blocked out Michael's most recent conversation with Dr. Whitney. He could not remember what he was supposed to do if the pain got this bad. He was only aware that the pills the doctor had prescribed were not working.

I've got to get home. He rose slowly from the booth. Suddenly, a burst of excruciating pain exploded in his head. He stumbled, knocking over the little table in front of him. The voices around him stopped and heads turned in his direction as he knocked over a second table in his attempt to leave. Michael put his hands up to his temples, trying to squeeze the pain out. It was agonizing. He had to get out of there.

He awkwardly made his way through the bar. The people around him stared as he staggered across the room. Several got up and started to follow him, taunting and jeering.

"Have too much to drink, buddy?" someone yelled.

"Can't hold your booze?" another voice chimed in. The crowd rippled with laughter.

Michael pushed through the sea of blurry faces. "Get out of my way!" he shouted, wildly thrashing his arms, trying to get past the gathering crowd that now seemed to block his exit. Finally, he made it to the front door. He stepped out onto the sidewalk, staggered a few more steps, and collapsed face down into the gutter.

The crowd had followed him outside. He felt one of the patrons lift his wrist to feel for his pulse.

The last thing Michael heard was a frantic voice above him yelling, "Quick, call 911. This guy's not drunk; he's dying!"

****

Making a quick call to her daughter, Catherine threw on whatever she could find and dashed to the hospital. Tamara and Ms. Nelson met her at the front doors and ushered her through the bustling hospital lobby into the administrator's private office.

"Please, sit down." Julianne Nelson motioned to the chairs on her right.

They each took a seat at the small table opposite the hospital administrator. The folder in front of her had Elliot's name on the tab.

"Can I get either of you anything?"

"No, no thank you," Catherine said. Tamara shook her head silently.

"Before we get started, I want to tell you how very sorry I am for meeting under these circumstances."

"Thank you."

"We just need a few signatures."

"Okay." She nodded.

Julianne opened the file and pulled out several forms marked with blue colored tags. "Please sign here," she directed Catherine, then swiftly switching the forms, "and here," she again pointed to the vacant line. A few more documents and they were done. "Thank you." After a final review to make sure everything was in order, she straightened the stack of forms and neatly placed them back inside the file and closed it.

The room was silent.

"Would you like to see him?" Ms. Nelson asked gently.

"Yes, I would." Catherine's voice cracked.

The three women exited the office. Catherine turned her head toward the front of the hospital, viewing the lobby; she could see the media had already begun to gather. The news was out.

They quickly made their way to the emergency room, successfully avoiding the intrusive reporters.

Emotions flooded Catherine, but she had to keep it together for the sake of her daughter.

Julianne stopped outside the double doors. "Mr. Paxton is just beyond these doors. I've notified the medical team you would be coming in to say your goodbyes. Do you have any questions?"

"No, I don't think so. Do you?" Catherine turned toward her daughter.

"No." Tamara shook her head, eyes glistening with tears.

"Okay, I'll leave you both here. However, if either of you need anything, please don't hesitate to give me a call. Again, I am so sorry for your loss."

"Thank you," the women quietly replied in unison.

Julianne excused herself and headed back in the direction in which they had come.

An alarm sounded as a gurney burst through the doors and rushed past them. It turned the corner and headed down the corridor, disappearing into the emergency room at the very end of the hall. Catherine watched in amazement at the precision orchestrated by the medical team on this patient's behalf.

"You go ahead, Mom." Tamara spoke first, breaking the silence. "I can say my good-byes later."

"Okay, sweetie." Catherine turned and slowly pushed her way through the double doors.

The stark white sheet had been turned down, making Elliot's head and shoulders visible. She slowly moved toward him. The medical team backed away giving them some semblance of privacy. He looked as though he were sleeping. Catherine touched his cheek. He was cold. His face was relaxed, reminding her of how he looked so many years ago when they were in love. No longer were there any signs of anger or hatred that had been so recently displayed. Unable to contain her feelings of overwhelming sadness, she gently laid her head on his chest and sobbed. Without thinking, she reached up and softly ran her fingers through his thick graying curls for the very last time.

Chapter 8

Michael's body lay lifeless. Only the rhythmic beeping of the monitors made anyone aware of life within the tiny room. Dr. Whitney's stocky figure could be seen coming and going at all hours of the day and night.

Dr. Whitney had made room 508 off limits to everyone, including the intensive care staff, which usually ran this wing of the hospital. He had brought in a specialized nursing team to care for this particular patient.

He knew that rumors had begun to run rampant throughout the hospital. He had heard them. Who was the patient and why was he here? Was he a diplomat or a foreign leader? So many unanswered questions...and nobody was talking. The added tension of dealing with such an unusual situation had everyone on edge, but once a gag order was handed down by the hospital administration, curiosity almost reached the point of being unbearable.

Inside room 508, Dr. Whitney was painfully aware of Michael's critical state. With all the tubing and wires surrounding him, he began to doubt himself for the first time in his career.

Did he just play God with someone's life? If word leaked out, the ramifications of this operation were beyond even his comprehension. He believed that what he had accomplished was done in the name of medical science, nothing more and nothing less. Or was it?

Dr. Whitney had devoted the past eighteen years of his life working on his theory. He was convinced that with the right procedures, brain cell grafting could prove very beneficial. He spent endless hours refining his technique. At first he utilized fetal embryonic brain cells and when he felt secure enough, he practiced on laboratory animals with tumors located in specific regions of their brains. In time the consistent displays of positive responses more than proved his theory not only to be correct, but with it came the potential to open doors to new fields of study.

Over the next few years, he became extremely proficient in his technique. He was confident that if he operated on a human the outcome would also be successful.

Then, as if by some random twist of fate, he was presented with Michael's case. Michael's unique medical condition revealed him to be a prime candidate. He believed he was being offered the perfect opportunity to prove his theory and recognized he would regret any decision other than the one he had made.

Dr. Whitney looked at the clock on the wall and sighed. He had been at Michael's bedside for the past four days, yet there were still no outward signs of life. There should have been some kind of a response by now.

Suddenly he felt extremely tired. *Well, it's out of my hands now.* He turned away from the bed and walked quietly out of the room.

He signaled to one of the specialized nurses on

duty. "Let me know if there are any changes." He gave this same order each and every time he dared to leave the room, even for a couple of minutes.

"Yes, Doctor."

Turning his back to the nurse, he headed slowly down the dimly lit corridor to the small office he had secured within the hospital.

****

With his head in his hands he appeared to be dozing, but he was not. Dr. Whitney could see that daylight had crept through the cracks of the half-drawn blinds, making a zebra-like pattern on the desk in front of him. His mind was locked into a continual re-creation of each and every move that had taken place in the operating room.

Hour after hour, Dr. Whitney scrutinized every aspect of the procedure. A tumor had developed on the outer surface of Michael's cerebrum—not very large—but the combination of the tumor's location and its recent growth spurt had caused Michael's last episode of excruciating pain, ending with his loss of consciousness.

Within minutes of his arrival, Michael's body was wheeled directly into the emergency room at the end of the hall. Dr. Whitney had no other choice but to operate. Something deep inside him told him this was a chance of a lifetime, his chance. No other decision was needed if he were to save Michael's life.

He deftly cut through Michael's scalp and drilled a small hole into the skull. He then inserted a small, thin tube-like instrument, immediately freezing the tumorous area. He cut carefully into the gray matter of the cerebral cortex, removing the tumor, and then grafted healthy cells from a similar area of the donor's brain. The operation took eight extremely intense hours and several skilled hands to complete.

Dr. Whitney had personally built the ideal surgical team. He interviewed, screened, and had each sign a letter of confidentiality. Every team member had a specific role in the delicately balanced operation and because they were on call twenty-four hours a day, they were housed in special living quarters right in the hospital. He made sure that every member was intensely aware that it was only a matter of time before their expertise would be needed in the operating room.

At the precise moment Dr. Whitney pulled his bulky frame up from the comfortable mold of his black leather chair, its familiar squeak was drowned out by the loud buzz of the intercom. The unexpected sound startled him. Slightly unnerved, he reached down and pushed the button.

"What is it?" he barked.

"Doctor, the patient in room 508 is showing signs of consciousness." The voice cracked through the speaker with unconcealed excitement.

"I'll be right there!"

****

The first thing Michael was aware of was an intense ache and a thick layer of bandages encircling the top of his head, continuing halfway down his face. Other than that, he couldn't remember anything.

"Michael?"

Tilting his head, Michael paused.

"Michael?"

The voice was familiar. Michael opened his mouth to answer, but the sound that came out was so hideous it startled him. He attempted to clear his throat and try again. With intense determination, he was able to force out a barely audible, "yes."

"Michael, this is Dr. Whitney."

Michael pursed his lips together, struggling to say something. After several frustrating attempts, he put his hands tentatively up to the bandaged area of his head.

"Don't try to talk right now." Assuming Michael's question, Dr. Whitney asked, "Are you asking if the operation worked?"

Michael slowly nodded, causing the ache to intensify.

"Well, we won't know how much of a success we have attained right away. Progress may be slow, but you being alive, conscious, and trying to communicate, I would dare to say we're definitely headed in the right direction."

Dr. Whitney pulled a small, gray plastic chair up to Michael's bedside. He sat down and continued.

"Michael," he said solemnly trying to mask his excitement, "I have to run a multitude of tests on you and by the end of the first series, I anticipate having enough information to form a preliminary prognosis. But as of right now, all I can say is that it appears the area of your brain that was operated on has not sustained any severe or, hopefully, lasting damage and is beginning to regain some of its' normal function."

The doctor paused and fidgeted uncomfortably in the small chair. "You know," he said slowly, "it really was just a matter of pure luck...and perfect timing that your operation was possible at all. He went on trying to fill in answers he might be asking if he were in Michael's position. "A donor became available due to a fatal automobile accident. As it so happened, which in itself is quite unbelievable, the two of you arrived at the hospital within, I'd say thirty to forty-five minutes of each other. We proceeded with the operation and basically here you are." Dr. Whitney stood up. "Well, that's enough for now. I'll be back in an hour or so to check in on you."

Exhausted by the brief exchange, Michael quickly slipped into a troubled sleep as Dr. Whitney gave all the monitors one final check before he left the room.

Chapter 9

The day had turned cold and gray, and a slight drizzle remained from the early morning rain. Catherine and Tamara stood close to each other, as if their closeness would ease their pain. Family and friends stood together, encircling the grave site. The cemetery grounds, both inside and out, were packed with people.

Catherine looked across the open grave and into the faces of many long-time employees of Scottford Textiles. She also spotted several of Elliot's business associates. She had a feeling many were there not out of sympathy, but merely to be seen, hoping that in some way their appearance would benefit them.

Of course, there was the ever-present press. They came in droves, one not wanting to be outdone by any other. Like all media events, be it public or private, the always curious were right behind them. Most stood just beyond the fenced grounds, as if coming directly into the cemetery would be testing the fates a little too much.

****

Standing motionless, Stephanie scrutinized the two grieving women. She had never seen the two of them together, and at this distance, it was hard to tell which of the two was older. She experienced a strange mixture of superiority and sadness for the women whose husband and father she had so intimately shared. Lost in her own thoughts, she didn't hear the conclusion of the service.

Suddenly Stephanie noticed people were moving away from her and she was no longer hidden. Panicking, she quickly turned and headed toward the main gates. She had stayed too long, and she had to get out of there fast.

Weaving through the crowd, paying little attention to where she was going, Stephanie walked directly into the back of the woman in front of her. As Stephanie mumbled an unconvincing, "I'm sorry," the woman turned and she found herself looking straight into the face of Catherine Scottford Paxton. Glancing sideways, she noted Tamara intensely watching the accidental encounter.

Horrified, Stephanie hurriedly made her way around the two women, fled through the open gates and down the block, never once looking back. If Catherine had recognized her, her expression had given nothing away, not even in those crystal blue eyes that seemed to look right through her.

She was out of breath when she finally made her way back to the car. She looked around, grabbed the handle, and yanked the car door open.

"Something wrong, dear?" a sarcastic voice asked.

His expression gave nothing away, and his eyes were shielded by the mirrored sunglasses he always wore. She could see…no, she could almost feel the loathing he felt for the man who had just been buried, the man he had once called his father.

Chapter 10

As she rode silently next to Garrett, Stephanie recalled the scene that had played out the night Elliot died. It was surreal. She had been waiting for Elliot to return from the airport debacle with Catherine, but it was Garrett, not Elliot, who showed up pounding frantically on her door.

As Stephanie unlatched the lock and opened the door, Garrett rushed past her, talking so fast she could hardly understand him. She stood there stunned, caught off guard by his untimely arrival.

"You've got to get out of here!" She tried to push him back toward the front door. "Elliot will be here any minute!"

"No, he won't," he said, easily stepping around her.

"There was a fatal car accident on the bridge and unfortunately it was Elliot. How sad." He made a quick unconvincing frown. "But God, don't you see how much easier this will make everything for us?" Garrett's voice rose with excitement listing each detail.

"What are you talking about?" Stephanie interrupted his rant.

"Don't you get it?"

"No. I...I really don't."

Exasperated, Garrett slowly and calmly repeated everything he'd said since coming through the door.

"Wait, you're talking about Elliot...Elliot, your father?"

"Yeah, and so?" He cocked his head and raised an eyebrow.

"He's dead?"

"Yeah."

"He's actually dead?"

"Yep." Turning away, Garrett calmly lit a cigarette and continued on as if they were talking about the weather. "God, this is the break we've needed for so long. Now, all we've got to do is get in and get everything we can as fast as we can!"

He looked back at Stephanie.

"I'm pretty damn sure my family will want to avoid even the slightest hint of public scandal. Since all of my life I was spoon-fed that scandal is *bad for business*," he imitated the sing-song voice.

"And this one little document could trigger a very long and intensive investigation and the result...scandal." His smile told her that once again he was confident he held all the cards.

"I figure with the right amount of pressure they will most likely offer you a generous settlement to keep you quiet about the affair...and any other information Elliot may have inadvertently shared with you between the sheets."

Stephanie cringed at the unnecessary insult.

"Hmmm...and your asking price; what do you think your asking price should be?"

She didn't respond, but her look of shocked disbelief was answer enough.

"Well, I think it should be double the amount sitting in Andorra. Yep, that sounds about right."

Stephanie was speechless. Slowly, she began to grasp that he was actually describing the accident which had claimed the life of his father. Not only that, but how his death would benefit their current situation.

She wasn't prepared for the cold and calculating person who stood before her. He appeared to be totally unaffected by this sudden turn of events. In fact, he seemed exhilarated by his father's fate. Stephanie didn't see even a hint of emotion that could be remotely connected to sorrow, and as she watched him, something inside of her shuddered in total revulsion.

Then as if nothing had changed, Garrett grabbed her, kissed her, and headed out the front door.

Stephanie glanced over at Garrett, noting his clinched jaw. *How did I let things get so out of control?* Her back stiffened as she tried to hold herself perfectly still in hopes that Garrett wouldn't be able to recognize fear he had created.

Chapter 11

Tamara stood quietly in the massive study that had belonged to her father. "Damn you. Damn you," she whispered in the empty room.

When Tamara and Catherine had arrived home from the funeral, the doctor was there waiting. Tamara quickly ushered her mother upstairs, away from the prying eyes of the servants. Without too much protest, Catherine allowed the doctor to inject her with a mild sedative.

Catherine had difficulty allowing someone else to take charge. But she had been through enough, and Tamara knew it was time to step in and take over. In a way, she was actually honored that her mother even allowed her to do so. With all that had recently happened, Tamara was satisfied she had made the right decision to temporarily move back home.

With her mother tucked comfortably in bed, Tamara saw the doctor out. Thanking him for his time, she softly closed the door and began wandering through the big house.

Everything was quiet as Tamara slowly walked down the main hall and through each room. She found herself picking up the intricate knickknacks her mother had placed around the house.

To strangers these items might be seen as priceless pieces of art strategically positioned to be seen at their best advantage, but to Tamara, they were much more than that. They represented a lifetime of memories, memories of happier times.

The sound of someone's throat being cleared behind her jolted Tamara out of her daydreaming. She whirled around to see Jeffreys, their butler.

"I did not mean to startle you, Miss Tamara. I just wanted to see if you needed anything."

"No, no; thank you," she said vaguely.

"Well then, Miss Tamara, I will retire for the evening. If you like, I will check on Mrs. Paxton on my way up."

"Thank you, Jeffreys. I would appreciate that."

"It would be my pleasure, Miss Tamara. Good night."

"Good night."

As the sounds of his footsteps faded, Tamara became painfully aware that she was standing in the middle of her father's study again. She needed to come to terms with how she felt about her father, and this was the best place to do it.

She had no false illusions; she knew her father for what he was, and working at Scottford Textiles, she was bound to hear the rumors. It wasn't long before she was made aware that her father had been cheating on her mother. Not just one or two affairs, but many. She was certain her mother was also aware, but if Catherine chose not to acknowledge them, then Tamara respected her silence. That was between her parents.

Still, it disturbed her that this last liaison had been going on for quite some time, and it was rumored to be serious, but Catherine never discussed it with anyone, so Tamara never questioned her.

Tamara looked up at the huge family portrait hanging on the wall behind her father's desk. What she saw were four people, three who were almost strangers to each other, and a fourth who worked so hard to keep harmony within these walls no matter what the personal cost.

She looked closer at the smiling face that so resembled her own. The only observable difference between them was the color of their eyes. Scrutinizing the multifaceted woman with the crystal blue eyes, she thought about all the trips they had taken to Europe. Tamara had turned to her mother for mentoring, amazed at her mother's knowledge of the entire corporation, even though she appeared to play no active role. Together, they spent many late nights discussing the business and its many competitors.

Catherine's opinions, insights, and concerns were so astute that Tamara recognized her mother was much more than a silent partner. She believed that her mother's quiet strength was what was truly behind the corporation's overall success. Through many long discussions they found that not only did they agree on many business-related issues, they agreed on a lot of things. It seemed as though there were very few times when they didn't agree...and as far back as Tamara could remember it had been that way.

During their visits abroad, they were wined and dined by the corporate heads of Scottford Textiles' sister companies. On each trip, Tamara and Catherine made an effort to discover something new: an out-of-the-way boutique, a new sidewalk café, or even a museum they had missed on a previous visit. No matter how tight their schedule was, they made a pact to see all that each city had to offer. It was always an adventure traveling with her mother, and Tamara loved these trips.

But on their last couple of trips, her mother was not her usual self. She was edgy and sort of distant. More than once she had begged off exploring someplace new, citing fatigue as the reason.

The more she thought about it, the more she began to pinpoint specific times in which Catherine had very discreetly excused herself. It was never obvious and was done with such finesse that no one around her ever seemed to notice her absence, not even Tamara.

Suddenly the pieces fell into place. Tamara understood what her mother was really doing. She had secretly remained an active part of the company's businesses all over the world, without her father knowing it.

"Oh my God!" Tamara whispered out loud. "This is incredible!" The realization renewed her admiration for her mother, but it also confused her. *How had she been able to hide this?* Her mother was so much more involved than any of them had ever realized, and Tamara was sure that was exactly the way she wanted it.

Stunned, Tamara crossed the room, heading directly for the bar. Though not much of a drinker, she grabbed the nearest bottle and poured herself a shot. In one swift movement she downed its contents, choking on the amber liquid. She poured herself another and took it over to the desk. She sat down in the massive chair, setting the drink aside, remembering just how bad it tasted.

Why didn't I catch on before now? Tamara was amazed that her mother had used their buying trips as a ruse to check on the company's holdings. This piece of information certainly shed some light on her mother's relationship with her father.

Tamara let out a long sigh. Her father…that was precisely why she was in the room to begin with. She slowly turned the big chair around until she was again gazing up at the handsome man in the picture. Did he have any inkling of how much his wife was involved in the running of the company? Probably not, she decided. Her father was too self-involved to have any idea of the power her mother wielded.

She continued staring at the picture, trying over and over—but no matter how hard she tried—she couldn't bring the thoughts of her father into focus. Maybe it was because their relationship was not as clearly defined as the one she shared with her mother; neither a bad nor a good relationship, it just was. Maybe she was looking too hard for something that wasn't even there. Pictures and memories began turning on and off in her mind. It was like watching old home movies that were poorly spliced together, with no correlation between age or time.

Tamara sat there for a long time, so immersed in making some sense of everything that it wasn't until his voice sounded in the quiet room that she knew she wasn't alone anymore.

"When no one answered, I let myself in," he said to the back of the big leather chair. "Somehow, I figured you'd be in here."

"What do you want?" she asked without turning the chair around.

"Is that anyway to greet a grieving family member?" His obnoxious laugh said it all. "Well, I just wanted to drop in and see how my two favorite ladies were doing."

Yeah, right, like a vulture dropping in on a rotting carcass. She didn't dare come right out and say it. She had decided a long time ago to stay out of it when things got turbulent between her father and her brother. This resolution was for her mother's sake. Where her brother was concerned, her mother had always fought an uphill battle with her father. Time and time again, Catherine had come to Garrett's rescue, both emotionally and financially. Her mother had always been there for both of them and Tamara knew she always would be, but it was Garrett who counted on it.

Their father had been too preoccupied to spend much time with Garrett as he grew up and her mother could not seem to fill the void it created. Tamara was fully aware that Garrett's destructive behavior was his way of trying to gain their father's attention.

It seldom worked, but when it did there was hell to pay for everyone.

For the first time, she felt as though his years of hatred were now aimed in her direction. Unjustly targeted, Tamara's self-control began to slip away.

"Like I said, what do you want?" Her jaw tensed. The tone of her voice should let him know he had overstepped his bounds.

"Nothing really, I…" He tried to back down, but she cut him off before he could finish.

"Why didn't you go to the funeral?" She knew her brother well enough to know that being questioned always made him feel as though he was being scolded. But this was not about him and she didn't really care what excuse he was going to use. She waited for his answer.

"He was a bastard, and you know it!" he yelled at the back of the chair.

"But you should have gone."

"Like hell I should have...and where do you get off telling me what I should do?"

Tamara turned the chair around. She leveled her gaze directly at her brother's face. There was no mistaking exactly how she felt.

"You could have gone for Mother's sake," she spat. "God knows how many times she's been there for you. Garrett, you're an ungrateful son of a bitch!"

Once the words were out, she immediately regretted it, but there was no way she could take them back.

Garrett's eyes narrowed. "You sound just like the old man. Well...at least we both finally know how you *really* feel."

The intensity of hatred behind Garrett's words sent a chill through her. She had struck a nerve that ran deep within her brother, but no matter what her brother did or if he even cared at all about the rest of the family, she knew he truly loved their mother.

"You know what dear sister, you're a fucking bitch!" Garrett yelled. He turned and headed out of the room toward the front door. Tamara followed him.

"Wait! Garrett I'm sorry!" *God, we don't need any more problems right now.* Tamara's mind raced as she made her way to the front door and out onto the front steps. "Garrett!" she yelled as he opened the driver's side of his bright red Lamborghini.

Garrett stopped. He turned toward her, his face visible from above the roof of the car. "Hey, let me know when they read the will. I promise I'll make it to that family gathering. Actually, I wouldn't miss that one for the world."

"Come on. Please," but he wasn't listening to her anymore.

As Garrett slid into the driver's seat, the interior of the car was bathed in light, and Tamara realized someone else was in the car. It was a woman, and she had watched the whole scene. Tamara had seen her before and it had been recently, but she couldn't remember where. As Garrett pulled his car around and down the long driveway, Tamara suddenly remembered; the woman had been at her father's funeral.

Chapter 12

"I'm sure she recognized me, Garrett. It's not like she's never seen me before," Stephanie hissed. "I told you we shouldn't have gone up to the house, but would you listen?"

"Shut up. I've got to think." The reaction from his usually reserved sister had definitely caught him off guard. And seeing Tamara sitting behind their father's desk had only infuriated him more. He couldn't help himself. Something inside him just snapped.

Garrett got up and lit another cigarette. He paced the small kitchen area of Stephanie's apartment.

"Okay now." He exhaled a long stream of smoke. "Okay," he repeated, trying to stay calm. "I know I blew it... Shit! Her seeing you with me changes everything. Damn it!"

He continued to pace, running his hands through his usually immaculately groomed hair. "I know that little bitch sister of mine will waste no time telling my mother about our impromptu visit."

Seeing Stephanie with Garrett would surely make his sister wonder what they were up to. Whatever Tamara was going to do with this new bit of information, they would now be headed for a battle that could ultimately cost them everything.

"Another fucking plan down the toilet." He stubbed out his cigarette with such force that it pushed the ashtray across the kitchen countertop, hit the floor with a loud crash, and smashed into pieces.

"Garrett!" Stephanie screamed. "Garrett, listen to me!" She crossed the kitchen floor, carefully avoiding the broken bits of glass, and firmly grabbed his arm. "Listen to me, please. We can't change the fact that Tamara saw me. If she goes to your mother, then we'll deal with it, but…" Stephanie's voice was now calm.

"Whether Tamara recognized me or not, she was going to find out anyway. There's nothing we can do about it now…and who knows? Maybe this will even speed things up a bit." Garrett didn't respond; he stared off in the distance, his face turned so that she could not fully see his expression. "Garrett?" she said softly, "Garrett, did you hear me?"

Garrett turned slowly until he was directly facing her. *Stupid bitch. You really don't know anything.* By the stunned look on her face and her body's involuntary shiver he could tell she was not expecting the murderous glare he aimed at her.

Infuriated, he didn't want his mother to know about them, at least not yet. He wanted to wait until some sort of settlement had been reached. Under these circumstances, his mother would not give in easily. Garrett secretly dreaded the disappointment he would see in his mother's eyes, he couldn't let Stephanie, or anybody, know how much he still wanted her approval. But now it was too late for that. Everything would have been so much better if he hadn't made such a stupid error in judgment today.

Elliot was dead, and now Tamara had seen Stephanie with Garrett. If Catherine became aware of their connection, Garrett would be unable to convince his mother to buy off Stephanie to be done with the whole messy affair. She would dig deeper, too much could be exposed, and he would get nothing.

"Knowing my mother as I do, there will be intense scrutiny over everything my father touched."

"Wait, let's think about this, maybe there's another way."

"The only way out of this will be to take my family's sterling reputation down...all of them."

A lifetime of bitterness was held in that single statement. It was as if Garrett had come face to face with all the anger and frustration he had held within himself for many years, and now he knew exactly what he wanted to do with it.

This was going to be a fight to the emotional death of everyone. Garrett felt more than justified in his decision because he had been emotionally dead for years. He no longer cared who got in his way. Now it was his turn to inflict pain on those who had stood by and let him suffer.

Through narrowed eyes, Garrett said, "But you're right, my dear. Tamara is just too smart for her own good. I will still take a shot at trying to get them to pay you off, but more than likely she will figure out who you are...her father and brother's whore. And if she does, then there is only one thing left to do." His icy stare held a silent threat.

Then abruptly, he announced, "I'll be back later," his voice returning to normal. There was not even a trace of the menacing figure he had just been. He regained his composure and was the picture of self-control. But it was too late; he had revealed the demons that possessed him.

Chapter 13

Stretched out on the soft wool blanket, he could smell the freshly cut grass. He heard the light laughter of someone beside him and turned to see who it was.

He saw the shape of a young woman with her back to him. She was busily unpacking a large picnic basket and spreading its contents neatly on the blanket before them. He watched her for a few moments, and as he did, a sense of urgency overtook him. He needed to see her face. He sat up, reached out, and gently touched the woman's shoulder.

"Yes?" As she turned toward him, her soft blonde hair brushed across the top of his fingers.

"Yes," the voice repeated. "I know this is an ungodly hour to check your vitals, Michael, but it'll only take a couple of minutes." Nurse Palmer said as she expertly went about the monotonous routine.

"Now let me get a little of your blood and I'm gone."

Michael felt the needle slip into his arm, and within minutes, he knew he was alone again. In the darkness he could picture the young woman with the silky blonde hair. She seemed so real. He lay there trying to re-create this latest image, but he could not.

Michael was getting extremely frustrated with these dreams. They appeared out of nowhere, and each time the same young woman was in them. He could not place her in either his past or his present, but it was obvious there was some kind of connection between the two of them. He didn't know how this could be possible when he couldn't even remember who she was.

"Damn it, who are you?" he said out loud. "And why can't I remember you?"

He tried to think back, but he always got stuck on the day he regained consciousness and heard Dr. Whitney's voice through the fuzzy cocoon that surrounded him.

Michael remembered the medical team converging on his room, removing all the life supports that had sustained him. Over the next couple of days, all the precautionary monitors were also removed. He had made extraordinary progress in such a short time that Dr. Whitney considered it something just short of a miracle.

Though his eyes and the upper portion of his head remained bandaged, Michael continued to grow stronger. He was allowed to walk around the small hospital room, but never outside of it. There were two remaining routines. One was physical therapy, which took place in his room because of the confidential nature of his case. The other was the constant check of his vital signs, done every two hours like clockwork, including several scheduled interruptions during the night. Not that it really mattered; he couldn't tell if it was day or night anyway, except by the meal he was being served, and with his currently prescribed diet, even that predictable gauge was sometimes questionable.

With the constant vigil surrounding him, his dreams were always interrupted. He had yet to reach the end of one. At this point, he wasn't sure there was an end.

He rolled over, trying to make himself more comfortable in the small bed. He could not get back to sleep. He kept thinking about the next day but dared not admit even to himself how anxious he really was. He was fully aware of the importance of each step in the experiment.

However, on the following day the medical team would be discussing the results from the most recent battery of tests. From these findings, they would come to some kind of consensus regarding the removal of the bandages from his eyes. He had heard through the ever-present rumor mill that several of the doctors had doubts that his bandages would be coming off anytime soon, but Michael remained positive, believing they'd be removed in a day or two.

For the first time since the operation, he would be able to match the voices to the faces of those who had taken care of him. Michael had made it a point to learn who was in the room with him, first by their voices and then later on by the sound of their footsteps. He had gotten so good that it became a game he played with the attending staff. When they entered the room, he had less than ten seconds to guess who they were while they busied themselves with their tasks.

Some of the staff had attempted to wear different types of shoes to try and fool him. Even with this little trick it only took him a few seconds longer, and he was usually right when he guessed who it was. The next day, though, he was positive there would no longer be a need to play this game.

****

Right after breakfast a light knock sounded at the door. "Come in. Oh, it's you, Dr. Whitney," he said before the doctor had taken more than four steps into the room.

Dr. Whitney chuckled. "Yes, it's me. And how are you doing today?"

Michael did not like the sound of the doctor's voice. He could tell it wasn't the news he wanted to hear.

"Not good news, is it?"

"I'm afraid not. After a long discussion, the team unanimously decided that allowing too much stimuli in before the brain is ready to process it could create serious, if not irreparable damage. To put it in the simplest of terms, something like a sensory overload could result."

The corners of Michael's mouth turned down in disappointment.

"Basically, Michael, they didn't want to risk any type of setback that might be caused by something as preventable as early exposure." The doctor paused. "I'm truly sorry."

"I see."

"You are making such extraordinary progress we're not willing to rush into anything that might put you at risk. We have all the time in the world. Actually, there is some good news in all this."

Michael leaned forward and tilted his head, listening with renewed interest.

"Because you are doing so well, we're moving you to a private rehabilitation center so you can continue on with physical therapy for the remainder of your recuperation."

"I'm glad I'm doing well, though, if I'm being honest, I'm not very happy about the decision to leave the bandages on. But I understand it."

"I'm glad you understand the need to proceed with extreme caution. Do you have any other questions?"

"No, I don't think so."

With nothing more to offer, Dr. Whitney said he would stop by later and excused himself.

He heard Dr. Whitney's footsteps as he exited the room. He sat patiently, waiting in total darkness, not knowing exactly what he was waiting for. He yawned, his body beginning to relax and soon he fell asleep. Within seconds, she was again there; he could almost see her face clearly this time.

She was smiling.

Michael slowly approached her. As he got closer, her face changed. She was no longer smiling. Stopping just a few feet away from her, her blue eyes revealed the most intense look of hatred he had ever experienced in his life. He raised his hand and started to call out to her, but as he did, she turned and fled as if she believed he intended to do her harm.

****

Within days of the team's decision to keep his bandages intact Michael was quietly moved from the private wing of the hospital to a secluded rehabilitation center. Day after day his routine was the same. He got up, had breakfast, and went to physical therapy. Then came lunch, more physical therapy, dinner, and ending his day with a shower…all done in darkness.

Michael's sporadic dreams of the young woman began as pleasant escapes from his present state of reality, but as time passed, the dreams became more frequent, longer in duration, and increasingly vivid. They no longer seemed like dreams, but more like memories. He could now envision her face whenever he chose to do so. Yet even with this ability, he could not place her anywhere in his life.

Lately, the dreams appeared to change time frames. The young woman had matured. She was now older than Michael and she was even more beautiful to him than when the dreams had begun.

The pain displayed so many times in those crystal blue eyes had turned to an intense loathing, her emotional turmoil growing each and every time she now appeared.

Michael believed her feelings were genuine, but he could not figure out why he affected her in this way. He was positive he was not the cause of these emotions. He felt as though he was on the outside looking in on someone else's life.

Chapter 14

He stood up, shaking his head as he folded the day's newspaper into precise sections. Passing through his immaculately kept apartment of black, white, and chrome into the minimally adorned kitchen, he opened the cabinet door under the sink and placed the perfectly squared bundle of newspaper in the recycle bin. He stood up, straightening his thin black tie and making sure it laid perfectly centered on his crisp white shirt.

He reached up and pulled out a white china teacup and antique silver tea strainer from inside the cabinet, absentmindedly rubbing his fingers over their entirety to make sure they were absolutely clean. Satisfied, he filled the top part of the strainer with dark strips of his favorite blend of imported English Breakfast tea and placed it directly atop the delicate cup. Setting the kettle on the right front burner, he leaned against the cool granite counter, patiently waiting for the high pitch signal that the water was ready. Already knowing the precise moment the hot kettle would sound, he carefully lifted it off the stove just as it started to whistle and poured the hot liquid on top of the loose tea, watching as the water slowly seeped through the leaves into the cup below.

This was his favorite part of the day, quiet and new. Conviction and order, all that anyone needed, which is exactly how he chose to live his life and pursue his profession. With the cup secure in his hand, he walked to the glass wall that overlooked the tops of the city's buildings. The deal had been made. Sipping his tea, he contemplated the task ahead of him.

When finished he took the cup into the kitchen and scrubbed it clean, then carefully placed it in the top rack of the dishwasher in its designated slot right behind the neat row of each day's used cup. He closed the dishwasher and tightly latched the lock. The sun had risen above the tops of the buildings and now shined unobstructed through the glass wall hitting the shiny black object that openly lay across the small kitchen table. He walked over to the table and picked up the AI AS50.

****

Catherine and Tamara sat at the large kitchen table, neither one talking much. Sitting together with a warm cup of coffee was comforting in itself.

"Well, I guess I should go down to the office and start clearing out your father's things."

"Oh, Mom, don't go. I'll take care of it. Really, I don't mind."

Catherine was relieved.

"Okay, then I think I'll stay here and finish up the thank-you notes for all the flowers and donations that were sent in your father's name. I know he would have found it amusing to see all the people who pretended to give a damn."

Seeing her daughter's reaction to her uncharacteristic use of sarcasm, Catherine placed her hand on top of hers. "Tamara, sweetheart, don't worry about me. I'm all right, just a little tired. And I do need to spend some time on this."

"I can stay and help you."

"No, that's all right. You've spent enough of your time here with me. I really do need someone to go through your father's things. You know, sorting through everything in his office is not much better than staying here. I appreciate your offer, though." Catherine hesitated, then decided to continue. "His office is going to need a good cleaning since it's now going to be your office."

Catherine watched as her daughter began to understand the meaning of her words. Tamara's eyes changed from a deep sea green to a bright shimmering green, and as Catherine had predicted, she accepted the offer with a mixture of pain and pride so easily displayed on her face.

"Are you sure this is what you want?"

"Yes, this is not only what I want, it is also what the Board of Directors wants as demonstrated by their unanimous decision yesterday!" Catherine had absolutely no doubts in her ability to run the company. The two women hugged each other tightly.

"Now off with you," said Catherine, trying to lighten the mood. "You have lots of work to do, and so do I."

The emotional tension broken, Tamara excused herself from the table and headed upstairs to her room to change. Within minutes she was back, dressed in camel-colored slacks and a cream silk blouse, her shoulder length blonde hair pulled back in a ponytail.

"Are you sure I can't help you today?" She asked, poking her head into her mother's brightly decorated office.

"No, dear." Catherine looked up from the pile of

unanswered mail. She smiled at her daughter. It still amazed her when she looked at Tamara, except for those beautiful, expressive green eyes, their likeness was startling.

"Okay. I won't be gone long, Mom."

"Okay," Catherine mumbled, already so intent on her task that she barely took notice of her departure.

Chapter 15

"Well, the time has finally arrived for these to come off." Dr. Whitney gently snipped and peeled the bandages away from Michael's eyes.

Michael was stunned by the brightness that surrounded him, even though every precaution had been taken to dim the room as much as possible. As his eyes adjusted, there were faces, many faces. The entire operating team, nurses, and a bevy of medical assistants had assembled in his room.

He looked from face to face, struggling to focus and comprehend what was going on. They all looked dismayed. Something was terribly wrong. He started to speak, but as he did, one of the team members signaled for him to stop.

A huge lump rose in his throat and he tried to brace himself for what was to come. He stared at them in silent apprehension.

"Michael," came the solemn voice from the man who had held up his hand. "Congratulations!" He cheered and lifted his other hand, which held a magnum of champagne. With that, the entire team burst into applause, followed by some tears and a heartfelt toast to Michael's recovery and their success.

After a lot of hand shaking and back patting, they said their goodbyes and left the small room. Only one person remained behind, standing next to Michael's bed.

"Michael, you're doing fantastic."

"Thank you, Doctor."

"It shouldn't be too much longer before you're released, but you know you'll still have to check in quite often so that we can run some tests and keep an eye on your progress."

"I understand," Michael said, though his mind was preoccupied. He had to know what was causing those images. They were always there now, lingering just below the surface, somewhere between daydreams and reality.

"Doctor, I honestly feel I have a pretty good grasp of what the remainder of the recovery process entails, but…" He stopped, not knowing if he wanted to get into this. "But there appears to be one complication that we haven't discussed."

"What's that?"

"Well." Michael shook his head. "I don't even know how to describe what's been going on." He paused and then continued. "At first it was like having dreams…you know, the kind where people and places come from your imagination and are intertwined with your own world."

Michael looked to see if the doctor understood what he was trying to describe. He was surprised to see how intently the doctor was listening. He seemed to scrutinize every word that came out of his mouth.

"These dreams are no way connected to my life—not my past, or my present. They have changed from a soft dream-like quality to a higher intensity, emotionally charged images. They are so strong, that even though I know they should belong to me…they don't."

The doctor paused as if he were searching for the right explanation. "I believe this is just part of a natural healing process. The brain has been traumatized. Your body is still sending your brain unrelated impulses. At this stage, we cannot determine what your brain is doing with these impulses, yet according to your tests in every other aspect, your brain is regaining normal functioning."

Michael sensed that the doctor was being somewhat evasive, but he decided not to push.

"I believe this is a temporary condition, but I will do some research into what could cause these intense image manifestations," he said firmly, definitely closing the subject for any further discussion.

"Now, getting back to your rehabilitation plan, you need to increase the number of your physical therapy sessions," Dr. Whitney continued, but Michael did not hear any more.

There's something he's not telling me, but there is no reason for me not to believe him. He looked at the man who had saved his life. Giving him a chance to find out what could be causing this was the least he should do.

Chapter 16

Tamara sat on the floor surrounded by stacks of books and personal papers that had belonged to her father. She sighed as she looked over the piles she had organized. There was just too much to get through in one day. She finally decided to pack the rest of it up and go through it at home and sent Grace down to the mail room for some empty boxes.

Tamara had been in that same position on the floor for so long that her back was aching. She got up slowly and stretched, then crossed the room and looked out the window toward the skyline. She had never appreciated the breathtaking view this office had. She would enjoy working here.

She glanced down at her watch, surprised that it was already three-thirty.

"Miss Paxton?" The voice was accompanied by a light tapping on the door.

"Yes, come in."

Grace entered with one of the mail room boys trailing behind her. His arms were loaded down with boxes, some of them slipping from his hold.

Without hesitating, Tamara caught the ones that were falling. "We'll put these over here." She smiled at him, hoping to ease his embarrassment.

"Thank you," he mumbled, more toward the floor than to Tamara, and quickly disappeared out the doors.

Tamara and Grace looked at each other and laughed.

"Miss Paxton…"

"Call me Tamara, please."

"I know you didn't ask for anything, but I took it upon myself to bring you a little something." Grace's voice lowered. The older woman started to explain. "You've been working all day without anything to eat. I thought…"

"Thank you, Grace; that was very thoughtful of you. Here let me clear off a spot on the desk."

While Grace disappeared to retrieve the food, Tamara started putting things from the desktop into the large cardboard box which sat balanced on the big leather chair. When the desktop was finally clear, she again checked through the drawers.

"Oops, I must have missed this one." She opened the bottom right drawer and found miscellaneous tools, an unused tape dispenser, and a San Francisco Giants' game ball.

Tamara remembered her father standing over her making sure the ball purposely slipped from his hands into hers. Reaching for the ball now, it eluded her grasp and rolled to the back of the drawer.

Reaching deeper into the drawer, Tamara's fingers touched something cold. She grabbed hold and pulled out a black metal box. She looked at it curiously.

"Here we are," Grace said, reentering the office with a tray of miniature croissants, sliced cheese, fresh fruit, and a small pot of freshly brewed coffee.

Tamara looked up. "Oh, that looks delicious. I didn't realize how much I needed a break." She absentmindedly put the metal box in the open carton in front of her, and then placed it on the floor with the others.

Grace slid the silver tray onto the desk. Tamara sat wearily in the large chair, smiling her thanks as she poured herself a cup of coffee.

"If there's anything else you need, please let me know."

"I will," Tamara said. Grace quietly left the office, shutting the doors behind her.

As she picked at the fruit, she knew her mother had probably not eaten either. She reached over and picked up her cell phone.

"Hi, Mom, it's me."

"Oh, hi sweetie. I thought you'd be done by now."

"Yeah, I thought so, too; it's taken me a lot longer than I expected. So, how would you like to meet me here in the city for dinner?"

"That would be fun. Where would you like to meet?"

"Umm, let me think. How about Anthony's on Harbor?"

"Perfect."

After deciding on a time—seven o'clock—they hung up. Tamara reached for her purse to toss in her cell phone and saw the mail she had grabbed from the mailbox at home on her way to the office. *This is as good a time as any.* She pulled a fistful of envelopes from her purse. The very first one she opened was a copy of the invitation that had been sent out for the Scottford Charity Ball.

The original idea for the event had been conceived by her grandparents. Thomas and Nora believed it was their responsibility to give back to the community that had helped them prosper. One night a year, they encouraged their friends and neighbors to share in their feelings of generosity and good will by hosting a charity ball.

It did not take long to figure out that participation in this event was not a choice, but an expectation... especially if one wanted to remain a part of the family and in good standing with Thomas.

It was not only an important community event, it was Thomas' way of chasing old childhood demons that continued to haunt him. No one in the family would dare think of letting Thomas down. Every year, they all pitched in to make the ball a huge success for the Scottfords' chosen charity.

The ball was held each New Year's Eve with a specific theme. No one ever knew exactly how they would be requested to donate. This made for an evening of fun and festivities; the growing sense of anticipation and suspense could always be counted on to end the event with a stupendous climax. The ball remained a major topic of conversation for months after the occasion.

Tamara sat and looked at the invitation that she and her mother had designed. It was absolutely perfect.

On the front a crescent moon was delicately engraved in gold with the words, "The Sky Is The Limit," printed up the moon's rounded side. A single star twinkled next to it. With all that had happened, Tamara had forgotten all about the ball until she opened the invitation.

You are cordially invited to attend
The Scottfords New Year's Eve Costume Ball
The sky is the limit, and we wish to see
you open your hearts

for those less fortunate than we.

~*~

Friday, the thirty-first of December
On the eve of the New Year
Eight o'clock in the evening
Lexington Hotel—Grand Ballroom
San Francisco, California

~*~

The favor of a response is requested
Attire: Celestial Costumes

Tamara let out a sigh of relief, so glad that almost everything had already been taken care of. A few phone calls, a couple of costume fittings for her and her mother, and that was it.

Tamara hoped the event would bring her mother out a little bit. Not that she had totally withdrawn, but she needed a little shove to get her life back on track. No way would Catherine ever let the memory of her parents fade.

She slipped the invitation back into its envelope, confident her mother would be as pleased as she was with the results. She went back to opening the rest of the mail: a couple of sympathy cards, a few donation verifications, and something looking official.

The letter was from the law firm of Franklin White. She recognized the name and it was addressed to her mother. *Should I open it?*

"Oh well, things can't possibly get any worse." She carefully opened the long envelope, withdrew the letter, and read:

Dear Mrs. Paxton,

I wish to express my deepest sympathy at the passing of your husband. I know this is a trying time for you and your family, however, we need to meet, review, and settle any financial issues that have arisen due to his untimely passing. We at Franklin White and Associates wish to assure a seamless transition of assets. Please contact our office at your earliest convenience.

My deepest condolences,
Franklin White

Tamara's face flushed in anger as she reread Mr. White's letter. There should not be any issues surrounding the transition of assets. Something didn't feel right. *So much for things not getting any worse*, because as far as she was concerned they just had.

Tamara grabbed her purse and burst through to the outer office, startling Grace. "Miss Paxton, is everything all right?"

"Uh…yes. Grace, could you please have all the boxes delivered to the house. I'll take care of the rest later."

"Yes, ma'am."

"Thank you." Tamara stepped into the elevator, the letter still tightly clutched in her hand.

Chapter 17

"If my calculations are correct, the bomb has dropped on my family right about now," Garrett boasted as he lay naked, outstretched on the bed. He tilted his head up, exhaling a long stream of cigarette smoke. The cruel pleasure he was experiencing was evident. His entire body seemed to radiate vengeance. Everything he said, everything he did, now centered on his obsession with destruction.

Stephanie looked at him through her thick veil of sable lashes. Something was dreadfully wrong. The person beside her had become a total stranger.

Garrett continued. "I can see one of two things happening now. Of course, first, there will be a big powwow held behind closed doors at the prestigious legal firm of Mr. Franklin White."

His voice took on a sing-song quality. "And lo and behold, Mr. Franklin White, himself, verifies the document to be the real McCoy!" His voice then turned cold. "I believe Mr. White will push my mother to settle with us...I mean you, then and there, because his involvement is stamped all over this. Good old Elliot was not smart enough to have set this up by himself. I'm sure Mr. Franklin can also be "persuaded" to have my mother offer a big payoff, citing the avoidance of bad publicity for the company. To save his own ass, of course, he'll make the magnanimous offer to take care of it all, so that she is not exposed to such sordid details."

He stopped, his anger building. "But that all hinged on that one little miscalculation on my part…the likelihood that my almost fuckingly perfect sister would see us together before the settlement, which she did, and then takes it upon herself to inform my mother. Because if she did, the big payoff will definitely be off the table."

"Garrett, I can't do it." Stephanie's voice came out a mere whisper.

"You what?" He turned toward her, instantly enraged.

"I said, I can't do it."

He grabbed her by the arms, her pale skin instantly turning purple under his fingers. He yanked her up. Doubling up his fist, he pulled back his arm and hit her full force in the face, sending her sprawling to the floor.

"It doesn't matter if you can do it or not. You will do anything I ask you to do!" He yelled as he stood towering over Stephanie's crumpled body.

****

Catherine stood in the center of her bedroom reading the letter Tamara had handed her moments before. Tamara sat quietly, cross-legged on her mother's bed, watching intently, waiting for her response.

When Catherine finished reading, she looked over at her daughter, her face never revealing her pain. She knew Tamara was still sorting out her feelings about her father and she was not going to influence her in any way.

"What do you make of this?" Catherine chose her

words carefully.

"I don't know, Mom, but I think we need to find out as soon as possible."

"I agree, but there's nothing we can do about it tonight. I'll call Mr. White first thing in the morning. Whatever it means, I'm sure we can straighten it out."

"I hope so."

"Now, I think I'll have Jeffreys bring me up a cup of tea and call it a night. I think you should do the same."

"Okay, goodnight Mom." Tamara said, moving toward the door.

Her mother did not respond.

****

Michael recognized her familiar laughter, but this time it was different. He could feel himself getting angry, but he wasn't sure why.

"Why, you little bitch. No, I haven't moved my things out!" he yelled. "I'll have them out tonight! But this isn't the end of it, my dear. I've invested too much of my life for the company and it won't be easy getting rid of me! I'm going to take what is rightfully mine… and if you get in my way, I will use whatever means necessary to stop you!"

Michael bolted upright in the small hospital bed, his body shaking.

"My God," he said out loud. He wanted to kill this woman. *But why? What was she to him?* The questions went round and round, but he had no answers. He had never experienced such pure unbridled hatred in his life.

This was not making any sense. He had no history with her. Yet, somehow, their lives had become intimately entwined. All the images were leading him somewhere, he was sure of that. His instincts told him that something was going to take place in the not-too-distant future—something terrible. He needed answers and he needed them now.

Chapter 18

Franklin White had been a practicing attorney for over thirty-five years. It was common knowledge that no one wanted to be on the opposite side of the courtroom if Mr. White was handling the case. His colleagues viewed him as a real hard ass. He went straight for the jugular, the quick kill, no emotions involved.

His office walls were impressive; hung among the customary law degrees, he displayed numerous original paintings. His enormous bookshelf was overflowing with the usual law books as well as a hefty display of many leather-bound first editions, truly the mark of a man who was successful—very successful—at what he did.

He checked his Rolex: eight forty-five. In fifteen minutes the Paxtons would turn his office into a battlefield. He normally would not allow that sort of thing to go on in here, but in this specific case, it was unavoidable.

When he received Elliot's paperwork naming Stephanie the beneficiary of the offshore account, he immediately understood what a lethal document he had. He read through its contents, stunned, and immediately put in a call to Elliot. He could not understand why Elliot had not come to him personally. This had to be a mistake. What was he thinking?

Unable to reach Elliot, Mr. White went directly to the new associate who had drawn up the document. Without trying to alert any suspicion, he questioned her about the revisions, but all she could offer was that Mr. Paxton had stated he knew Mr. White was too busy to deal with something as trivial as a revision of beneficiary. Mr. Paxton had said he really needed it to be done right away. He had also mentioned something about major changes that were about to take place at the Scottford Corporation, but he had not elaborated.

He knew exactly why Elliot had not come to him personally. If Elliot had, he would have tried to talk him out of this foolish idea. But the damage had already been done, and now Elliot was dead. And actually, his recent death provided the perfect excuse for his associate to turn over the file of work she had done for Elliot without even questioning Mr. White's interests. She should be fired, but he needed this to be buried and quickly.

All Mr. White could do was put one of his investigators on the case to see if he could prove or disprove the authenticity of the document. Every instinct told him something was not quite right, but the investigation came up clean.

The signature was Elliot's. The postmark on the envelope had not been tampered with. The document itself had been drawn up in accordance with the law. It had to have been; it had been done by his very own firm.

The investigator did turn up some rather interesting information on Stephanie Angelina Delaney, the person named as the sole holder of the account. According to the report, Miss Delaney was having an affair with both

Elliot and his son, Garrett, and in fact, this cozy little situation had been going on for quite some time. And apparently, Elliot was unaware of his bed-hopping bunny's extracurricular activities.

Mr. White found the situation distasteful, but it did not by any means invalidate the document. He exhausted every imaginable avenue before resigning himself to the fact that a meeting of all family members was needed. He hoped to convince the Paxtons of the seriousness of the situation and potential dangers of this document going public. Even a hint of scandal and the company could take a substantial beating on the stock market. But, Catherine Paxton was smart, smarter than Elliot had ever given her credit for, and she would do the right thing for the company, but he had never dealt directly with their children.

The buzzer on the intercom sounded. "Mr. White, Mrs. Paxton and Miss Paxton are here."

"Show them in, Ashley."

Chapter 19

Dr. Whitney concluded his final evaluation. Everything checked out. He picked up the chart to make some last-minute notations.

"That does it," he said and snapped closed the metal clipboard. "You're ready to be released, Michael. We have an apartment all set up for you, not too far from the hospital, in case you need us. But you shouldn't."

Michael listened quietly.

"And even though you are being released, the nature of this operation is experimental, and the specifics will still need to be kept confidential."

Dr. Whitney watched Michael to see if any sign of confusion was present, but Michael obviously understood, so he continued. "You could experience things like nightmares, memory lapses or losses, seizures, or any type of complication that is directly related to brain trauma. In all probability, any of these complications could potentially happen as the brain continues to heal. Honestly, Michael we just don't know."

"I understand, and I am still in agreement with everything." Michael nodded.

"And I cannot stress this next point enough. At this time, you are not to use anything that requires direct or close contact with anything that emits even the slightest amount of radiation, which basically means no cell phones, computers, microwaves and oh...at least for now, no televisions either. Though great strides have been made in lowering radiation emissions, we just aren't sure what effect any emission could have on you. It could compromise the cells as they continue to heal, or we could see a slow rejection of the graft. To put it quite bluntly—it could cause your death." Dr. Whitney hoped he was getting through to Michael. "I'm really not trying to scare you; I simply want to stress how very important this is."

"I understand, Doctor, and I'm fully aware that I'm a human guinea pig who is now going to be living back in the 70s. Should be an interesting challenge." He chuckled. "But seriously, I realize that because of the risks you've taken, I'm still alive. And for that, I can't thank you enough. I will follow every one of your instructions to a tee. I won't risk any sort of exposure. I know that even a hint of controversy could hinder further research." He paused. "You have my word. Asking me to remain silent is a small thing, considering all you have done for me."

"Thank you, Michael." Dr. Whitney extended his hand, and Michael returned his grasp, both acknowledging they had sealed their mutual agreement of silence.

Briefly, Dr. Whitney's eyes filled with unshed tears. He cleared his throat and composed himself, returning to his professional demeanor. "Nurse Palmer will take you to your new apartment and see that you have everything you need. She'll spend several hours a day with you to monitor your progress, answer questions, and make sure you get to your physical therapy sessions. I want to see you one week from today, unless you need anything sooner. Please, don't hesitate to call me anytime, and I do mean anytime."

Michael laughed. "Okay, okay."

"Any questions?"

"Only one," he said tentatively. "I think I might also need some psychological help."

Dr. Whitney frowned. "Why is that?"

"The images."

"I see." Dr. Whitney let out his breath heavily.

"I know you said they should climax and then start to decrease, but I am honestly afraid of what that climax might be. I thought with therapy, I might be able to meet these images head-on and try to figure out what caused them to surface. If I know that, maybe they will go away, or I could possibly stop whatever it is from happening."

Dr. Whitney did not respond.

"I feel if I don't do something—anything—something terrible is going to happen. And somehow, I know I'm going to be right in the middle of it." Michael was visibly shaken.

"All right. I'll see what I can do," he said, finally breaking his silence.

Dr. Whitney didn't tell Michael there was absolutely nothing he would do at this juncture about the images. Whatever was going on inside of Michael's brain would have to play itself out.

"Anything else?" Dr. Whitney asked, trying to cover his uneasiness.

"No, I don't think so." Michael sounded somewhat reassured.

"Then go ahead and get dressed. Nurse Palmer will

be right in." The doctor forced a smile, hoping to convince Michael that everything would be all right.

****

"This is really nice, Nurse Palmer," Michael said. "And thank you for the tree," he added. A small potted Christmas tree decorated with miniature silver ornaments and tiny red bows on the end of each branch had been placed on top of the kitchen table.

"It was nothing," she said, blushing.

The apartment was small but clean. *So this is what radiation free living looks like.* He looked around several of the rooms, noting a void of all modern technology.

It might be small, but it was just the right size, Michael decided, considering he had disposed of most of his belongings once he had made the decision to go ahead with the operation. No matter what the probabilities were, Michael dared not hope he would ever fully recover.

The only things he kept were some boxes of books, his personal papers, and a couple of old photo albums. Looking down at them he was glad he did, realizing this was all that he had left of his old life.

When he found out that he was terminally ill, and with nothing left but an experimental operation as an alternative, he met with Dr. Whitney, who presented his theory and described the procedure. The doctor's premise was sound. All that was missing was someone who needed this type of operation and was willing to take the risk. Within the first few appointments, Michael figured he fit the bill pretty close and ultimately decided he had nothing left to lose.

The only issues that concerned Michael weren't

medical. It was Dr. Whitney's request that he have no serious relationships for at least a year, and once he began forming attachments he was to remain silent forever. He recognized the need for secrecy as the operation was still in the experimental phase, and even after Dr. Whitney had presented him with the possibility of a favorable outcome, his untrained mind could clearly see that there were no guarantees. Years of study were needed before an operation such as this would be accepted as a viable treatment for the brain. But forever was a long time.

Dr. Whitney had said intimacy would only complicate matters. He knew at some point in an established relationship, Michael would feel obligated to tell his significant other the truth. How else could he explain away weeks, maybe months of a disappearance if something went wrong? Of course, he couldn't. One honest disclosure and the experiment would be jeopardized and Dr. Whitney was just not willing to take the chance.

Once Michael agreed he recognized it would prove to be costly. He would have to give up his fiancée, Anne, his friends, and his current teaching career. Realistically, without the operation, he would not have these things in his life much longer anyway. On the other hand…he might just come out of this alive.

After a great deal of agonizing, he made a decision. He severed all his personal relationships, starting with the one that would be the most painful; his fiancée. He figured if he could survive hurting Anne, he could survive anything. She was stunned when he had broken off their engagement, but after weeks of getting nowhere with him as to why, Anne accepted his decision and moved on with her life.

Giving up Anne was one of the hardest things Michael had ever done and the anguish was as deep as when he had buried his parents within three months of each other.

Mapping out a plan to execute his departure from the university Michael started expressing a desire to find some small, out-of-the-way place that really needed him. He began taking short trips, sometimes extending his days off, saying he was looking for a place where he really wanted to teach. He had done this so often it had become an accepted fact to those around him that he would leave. It was just a matter of when.

When he finally revealed his decision to leave it was met with a surprising amount of admiration. He was truly shocked when he learned that many of his colleagues had the same urge as he did but had become trapped by the need to provide stability to those dependent on them. Michael was careful not to disclose any of his circumstances, even when his closest peers secretly expressed how lucky he was to be unattached at this stage of his life and to have the opportunity to start over. He didn't feel so lucky.

Chapter 20

Garrett strode cockily through Mr. White's outer office. He was late. When Ashley spotted him, she reached for the intercom to inform Mr. White of his arrival. But as she did, he quickly placed his hand over the button.

"No need, my dear," Garrett said sarcastically. "I'll announce myself."

He tilted his head to one side, leering at her well-presented cleavage. "Well, wish me luck." He withdrew his hand from the intercom panel, deliberately brushing against her left breast.

Ashley immediately drew back, disgusted.

"See ya." Garrett winked in her direction, turned, and disappeared into Mr. White's office.

****

"Sorry I'm late," he said nonchalantly as he entered the room.

Tamara turned and glared at her brother. Her instincts told her that he was somehow connected to the calling of this meeting. She didn't know how, but she was sure he would trip himself up, sooner or later, just like he always did when he got himself in too deep.

"It's all right, dear," Catherine said.

"Let's get started," Mr. White said, taking control of the meeting. "Please take a seat." He motioned to an empty chair in front of his desk next to Catherine and

Tamara.

"No thanks. I'll stand."

"All righty then, we need to come to some kind of agreement as to how you would like to handle the surfacing of your late husband's...umm...let's just say documented transgression. As you know, going public could be corporate suicide. I've seen it happen before." He shot a knowing look at each of them as he cleared his throat and continued. "Under normal circumstances, I would never recommend offering a settlement up front, but in this case, it is what I would advise you to do."

"What?" Tamara stopped, realizing she may have over stepped her bounds.

"Go on, Mr. White," Catherine said calmly.

Tamara looked at her mother in disbelief. She had assumed that they would fight whatever was thrown at them. That's what the Scottfords had always done. The company had weathered many storms and had proven to be strong enough to withstand any type of accusation without jeopardizing the investors' profits. But with the threat of Elliot's personal indiscretions being exposed, Tamara saw her mother wavier.

"I feel that the best plan of action is to offer the young woman a generous settlement. Do it quick, no questions asked and hopefully no one, including the press, will catch wind of it." Mr. White went on, his voice tone as smooth as if he was offering his closing argument in court on a case he had to win. "By making this young woman an offer, she gets what she wants and we avoid all the negative publicity that could ultimately cost the corporation millions."

"I agree with Mr. White," Garrett said looking

straight at his mother. "Our family has been through enough crap to last us a lifetime. Let's pay her and get it over with."

Tamara sat silently and scrutinized her brother's charade. She could not believe what she was hearing. There was no way her greedy brother would voluntarily give a strange woman money that was destined to be part of his inheritance, unless it would in some way benefit him. It didn't make sense. "Excuse me, Mr. White," Tamara said quietly. "What did you say the lady's name was?"

Garrett had been talking to his mother and stopped in mid-sentence. He turned and looked at his sister.

"Does it really matter who she is, Tam?"

"No, it really doesn't matter, Garrett. I just want to know who she is." Everything about his body language told Tamara there was some sort of connection.

"You know her, don't you?" Her eyes changed to a deep forest green as she challenged him. Whatever instinct was driving her forward, she knew she was right on target.

Mr. White started to intervene, but Catherine motioned for him to stop. She whispered, "It's time for them to work things out for themselves. Our family has been shaken down to its very soul. Their issues need to be part of the settling dust."

Mr. White and Catherine remained silent as Tamara and Garrett began to battle.

"No," Garrett said, responding to Tamara's question. "I mean... I know she was one of the models employed by the company."

Tamara could tell it was taking every ounce of self-control Garrett possessed to remain calm. She saw her mother's questioning eyes upon him. She decided to push forward just to see what they were truly dealing with.

"A model, huh?"

"Yeah, just a model." He shrugged his shoulders.

"Hmmm, so was she the one who was in your car the day of the funeral?"

"I didn't go to the funeral," he said, obviously trying to avoid the issue.

"At the house, Garrett...the house!"

Tamara saw Garrett look over at his mother and wince.

Catherine rose from the chair, crossing the room to him. "Garrett, what do you know about this, and I want the truth. For once, tell me the truth." Catherine almost begged.

Garrett shot a murderous look at his sister. "You little bitch. You've blown everything," he mumbled inaudibly and turned back to his mother. "Her name is Stephanie, Stephanie Delaney. We've known each other for a long time, and for a good majority of that time we've been sleeping together," he bragged. "And yes, she was sleeping with me and Dad at the same time; kind of kinky, huh?" he sneered.

Tamara saw her mother flinch.

"Pay her off or I promise it will only get worse! All she wants is the money, and she wants it now. It's as simple as that. Just *pay* her, Mother! Or I'll turn your precious little company upside down."

Watching him made Tamara sick to her stomach. She really wanted to speak up and hurt him with as much intensity as he was hurting their mother, but this was one of those times when it was best to stay out of it. Her mother was quite capable of handling him herself…at least Tamara hoped she was.

"Are you quite through, Garrett?" Catherine's voice was hard and cold, shocking both of her children. They had never witnessed their mother use this tone before.

"I'll give you five million dollars to make this all go away. This is far more than she…or should I say…you…deserve. So take the offer and get out of our lives. I don't want to see or hear from you ever again." The room fell silent.

Tamara was stunned at what her mother had just said to Garrett, the child she had so fiercely protected and defended all these years.

"A measly five million, Mother? I don't think so," Garrett responded, breaking the silence. "But I'll discuss it with Stephanie and get back to you." He smiled at her, but there was nobody recognizable behind the smile.

"Well, I guess this meeting is over," he announced flippantly, then turned and headed out of the office. "Catch you all later," he called over his shoulder as if nothing out of the ordinary had just taken place.

Catherine looked at Tamara. They both turned to Mr. White, who was staring dumbfounded at the door Garrett had just exited.

"Mr. White?" Catherine asked.

"Yes…yes." He looked at both women in resignation. "I hate to say it, but we will have to sit tight and wait until we hear if she will accept your offer or not…and let's hope that she does."

****

The sky had clouded over, and the day was dark as

a lone figure stood in the shadows of the Gothic pillars that graced the front of the building. He smiled as he watched the scene taking place before him.

Upon exiting the huge building Catherine and Tamara were immediately rushed by reporters with cameras flashing. He saw his mother instinctively step forward, trying to shield Tamara from the frenzy. In the commotion they linked arms, as Maxwell positioned himself in front of them, guiding them easily through the crowd, and into the waiting limousine. It was obvious their family dilemma was no longer a secret.

"I just wonder who could have possibly leaked all that information about today's little meeting?" Garrett smiled triumphantly. He leaned back against the smooth surface of the tall pillar and lit a cigarette.

Chapter 21

"So this is what you've been up to behind my back," he said aloud as he went over the investigative reports. His suspicions had been correct. She had quietly concealed the fact that she had a controlling hand in almost all of the company's interests, both in the United States and abroad. From the documents, it appeared she had been doing this all along.

He paced the room, something he did when he was angry. "How could I have been so blind?" he chided himself. Shit, I wonder if she knows about the offshore?

"Well, my dear, it is time to put an end to this little masquerade of yours." Again he flipped through the report, getting angrier as he did. He tossed it on his desk. He could not tolerate this deception, at least not hers!

She had the power to make him the laughing stock of the company...if she hadn't already done so. This absolutely infuriated him. "I cannot allow this to continue," he shouted. By rights the company belonged to her, but he had worked too damn hard to let her get away with it. He walked back to the desk, picked up the report, and read it again, so enraged that the writing blurred on the page. He squinted, trying to continue, but the harder he tried, the more blurred the page became. Frustrated he closed his hand, crushing the report.

"You're next, bitch!"

Michael looked down at his clenched fist and then scanned the room, confused. Nothing was there. He was at home, lying on his own couch. *I must have dozed off.* Michael looked at the clock. He needed to get ready for his appointment. He sat up, still feeling drowsy.

Flexing his fingers to relieve the stiffness, he remembered the images that had just filled his mind.

He knew now that the woman with the beautiful blue eyes had something to do with a very large corporation, that someone was not very happy with her, and that person definitely intended to do something about it.

Now when he closed his eyes, he could play back pieces of the images, but there was no sense of continuity. The more he tried to sort it out, the more complicated it seemed to get.

He decided to stop by and speak with Dr. Whitney after physical therapy. Perhaps he had found someone who would be willing to work with him under such stringent conditions.

Maybe it's nothing. Maybe I'm making too much out of all this. He tried to calm his mounting apprehension. But something inside him knew that whatever was going on, he would be a part of it and he would not have much choice in the matter.

****

Physical therapy was one of those agreed-upon conditions, remaining a constant in Michael's life. No matter where he was—first, the hospital, then the rehab center, and even now living outside the protective walls of a medical facility—he remained committed to the regimen. On Mondays and Wednesdays Michael did whole body workouts. Though they were tough in the beginning, he came to appreciate these sessions as they had turned his naturally lean frame into one that was now toned and well sculpted, something he never really had time for before.

On Tuesdays and Thursdays, he worked on his hand-eye coordination, utilizing toys to address his fine and gross motor skills, which sometimes made him feel like a child. He was asked to complete a variety of tasks from stacking blocks, putting shapes in their appropriate holes, stringing beads, or dressing and undressing dolls. Michael made his way from the big buttoned, zippered, and lace-up doll to the intricate dressing of Barbie and Ken.

Every other Friday he had what he liked to call mind games. This was his least favorite type of therapy and today was that Friday.

Nurse Palmer dropped him off and said she'd be back in three hours. He walked into the quiet office, signed in at the counter in front of a sliding glass window, then turned and took a seat in a vacant chair. It looked like there were only two people in front of him. *Good, the wait won't be too long.* He automatically picked up a magazine and thumbed through it.

His named was called.

Let the games begin. He got up and headed through the opened door and was ushered to the small room on his right.

"How's it been goin'?"

"You know, pretty much the same. So, what kind of game do you have for me today?"

"Oh, you're gonna love this one."

"I'll bet." Michael smiled at the young therapist.

"Okay, let's get started. First let me explain, I have chosen this particular exercise to work on your memory connections in hopes that your past memory has integrated with your present memory."

"Okay. Sounds interesting."

"The area of your brain that was operated on is where we store memory...which you already know." Doug shrugged in apology. He continued.

"I'm going to conduct something like a guided visualization starting as far back as you can remember and then bring you slowly up to the present. You'll be hooked up to machines that will monitor your brain activity, along with your breathing and pulse. Nothing intrusive, kinda like what happens during a sleep study, but you'll be awake."

Michael was intrigued.

"I would like to accomplish two things with this exercise. First to see if the operation has caused any gaps in your memory and second, to get an approximate idea of not only your healing progress, but also the rate at which you are healing. I hope to be able demonstrate that your memory has in fact remained intact and gain enough information to project with some degree of accuracy the duration of healing from the time of the operation to the completion of healing." Doug smiled at Michael. "So, what do you think? Do you wanna try it?"

By the tone of his voice Michael knew Doug was really excited about this one.

"Sure. What do you need me to do?"

"First, I need to wire you up, if that's okay?"

"Well, I'm pretty sure my memory will check out okay, but I'm real interested in finding out what the projected end date of all this fun will be," Michael said as Doug placed wires on his forehead, scalp and chest.

After securing the wires, checking and rechecking the monitors, Doug seemed ready to go.

"Could I get you to lie down here?" He patted the examination table, and swiftly pulled out the leg extension at the base of the table.

Michael did as he was asked.

"Okay, just lie back and relax."

Michael lay back, put his arms up, locked his fingers together and placed his hands behind his head as Doug dimmed the lights and pulled the small round stool up to the table.

"Now close your eyes, take three to four deep breaths, inhaling and exhaling slowly with each breath," Doug instructed in a deep clear voice.

It took Doug approximately two and a half hours to guide Michael through his childhood, the loss of his parents, cutting all ties to his former life, up to the day when he had lost consciousness. The routine checking of the monitors confirmed that things were going well. Michael's brain appeared to be healing at the normal rate of any brain injury.

Satisfied that he had all the information he needed to make an assessment, Doug turned back to unhook the monitors. When he reached the monitor that recorded Michael's brain function the screen was alive with activity which would signal extreme agitation, yet when he turned back to observed Michael, he was lying quietly on the table.

There she was again standing right in front of him, her crystal blue eyes filled with tears and a hurt that could only have been caused by years of pain. Who are you? he wanted to ask, but no words came out. They both stood there staring in silence. Michael's body tightened, starting in his legs and moving up through his body until it seemed to rest between his shoulder blades. Knowing he could no longer stand in silence, Michael spoke. "I know I don't know you, but you are here, in my mind...I think?" There was no response. "Is there something I can do to help you?" he asked, hoping a question would invoke some kind of reaction. Nothing. Michael felt himself getting irritated by her lack of response. He didn't know why he was getting angry; she hadn't done anything to him. This is bullshit, the thought exploded in his head, so he abruptly took several steps in her direction. He was shocked at his aggression; he looked down at his own feet feeling as though something or someone else was moving him forward. In that brief moment he had taken his eyes off her, she disappeared just as quickly as she had appeared. He stood alone struggling to make some sense of what had just happened and what he could possibly do to stop it from continuing.

"Michael...Michael!"

He felt himself being shaken, as if someone was trying to wake him.

"Michael, are you all right?"

He could hear the concern in Doug's voice. "I'm okay." Michael tried to clear his head. "Really, I'm okay."

Michael slowly sat up on the table, his body tense. Doug quickly began to remove the rest of the wires.

"I don't know what the hell just happened here, but I've never seen anything like this before," Doug said, pulling off the adhesive that held the last wire in place.

"I'm not quite following; can you explain what you mean?"

"Well, when I did the final round of monitor checks for the conclusion of the session, both your mind and your body were reading in a complete resting state. But when I began detaching the wires on the monitors, the monitor that gauges your brain activity had suddenly gone berserk, I mean, like off the charts! But here's the weird part: you weren't moving at all."

Michael listened as Doug tried to explain what he already knew.

"Michael, uh, something really weird is going on and I honestly think you should see Dr. Whitney…like right away." His expression displayed genuine concern.

"You know, I plan to do just that." Michael tried to put the younger man at ease. He was convinced now more than ever that whatever was going on needed to be stopped, and it needed to be stopped quickly.

****

"I feel like I've been dropped right into the middle of someone else's life, Dr. Whitney. I can't even begin to explain to you how real everything feels."

The doctor did not respond. He sat, listening intently.

Michael continued. "Each time one of these images emerges, the intent to do harm to this woman intensifies. I'm really concerned. I feel like…" Michael could hear his voice rising. He stopped to gain his composure, and then continued, trying to lend credibility to why he had come.

"Anyway, Dr. Whitney, that's why I'm here. That and to see if you have found anyone who could work with me."

Dr. Whitney leaned back in his chair. "I haven't been able to find anyone who has the qualifications and can pass the rigorous background check, but I'll keep looking."

"Thanks, I'd appreciate that."

"But from what you're describing I believe you may be experiencing random thoughts or…you know, what people call wishful thinking; not that I'm saying you wish to harm anyone, but it could be an expression of some sort of pent-up anger that has manifested in this way. They might also be actual memories that you have suppressed or distorted."

"How will I know which one it is?"

"I really don't know. Because of the extreme newness of this operation we have very little information to go on."

The doctor paused, then his speech became rushed. "As a matter of fact, it is mostly speculation on our part as to what you are experiencing. We are learning from you. You are basically the only form of documentation we have right now, so please bear with us and continue to report everything you're experiencing. We need to know all that you're going through—physically, emotionally, and especially anything about these reoccurring images. That is a complication we had not anticipated. Everything is of importance to us. I cannot stress this enough. But at this point, I'm not seeing anything you should be overly concerned about."

"Okay." Michael wasn't sure whether the doctor couldn't or wouldn't explain further. Either way, Michael was on his own.

Dr. Whitney rose from his chair. Taking his cue that it was time to leave, Michael also rose.

"I have another appointment right now, but I'm glad you stopped by," Dr. Whitney said. "Our regular scheduled appointment is...let me see"—he casually flipped through his calendar—"on Tuesday."

"Right." Michael said, a little uncomfortable, as if he wasted Dr. Whitney's time with something so trivial. "Sorry if I inconvenienced you, by just dropping in."

"No problem at all. You can come by anytime. You know that."

All the words were the right ones, but somehow the feeling didn't follow. Dr. Whitney came from around his desk as if to usher Michael out of his office. Michael could hear his words of encouragement even as he exited the office.

****

Alone in his office, Dr. Whitney took a deep breath and shook his head. He hated lying to Michael, but he had to. According to the limited research on the effect of brain cell grafting he discovered there was more than a strong possibility that Michael's images were bits and pieces of his donor's memories and they were leading him to events that would take place in the future. He theorized that was why the intensity had increased. If the events had already taken place, the frequency and intensity of the images should logically have diminished. There would be no psychiatric care.

Michael showing up without an appointment was so uncharacteristic it was clear sign he was getting caught up in whatever was taking place. *I can't risk telling him the truth.* The doctor appreciated Michael's good intentions, but he could be placing himself at risk, as well as jeopardizing the experiment to exposure.

Dr. Whitney envisioned the chaos it would create if

the details of the operation were prematurely leaked. He would not allow all his years of hard work to be misused in any manner or for any reason. He was determined to have his test case run its full course uninterrupted. He would take whatever steps necessary to secure its secrecy.

****

Michael was disappointed the visit had not given him the clarity he so badly wanted. The sense of urgency still lingered. How would he be able to find the unknown blue-eyed woman without any more information than he already had, and how could he possibly make inquiries without calling too much attention to himself?

Whatever he did, he would have to be careful, extremely careful.

Michael was now totally convinced that Dr. Whitney would not be giving him any information, so that avenue was definitely closed. The more he thought about it, the more challenging it became. He smiled. He rather liked the idea of a good challenge, though not naïve, he realized this challenge could possibly cost him his life or maybe the life of someone else.

He walked into the waiting room, where Nurse Palmer sat patiently.

"Ready to go?"

"Yep, all finished," he replied, already busy formulating a plan. He knew exactly where the beginning of his search would take him.

Chapter 22

Catherine had not said a word during the drive home. The mob scene in front of the lawyer's office was too much for her. Once home, she headed straight to her room without speaking to anyone.

Tamara changed into jeans and a loose-fitting work shirt. This was how she really preferred to dress. She had tried to read but found she could not concentrate. After reading the same page for the fourth time, she put down her book and headed to the kitchen. She busied herself preparing sandwiches to take up to her mother.

Standing at the spotless counter, Tamara thoughts turned to Garrett. *What was wrong with him? What was he thinking? How could he do this to their mother? She had supported him each and every time he had gone head to head with their father. Couldn't that idiot see what he was doing to her?* She had never seen her mother like that before. The tone of voice she had used in Mr. White's office still echoed in her ears.

Finishing up, she placed the sandwiches and some Perrier on a silver tray and headed up the stairs to her mother's bedroom. The door was slightly ajar. Tamara knocked lightly.

"Yes?"

"Mom, can I come in?"

"Sure, sweetheart."

Tamara entered the dimly lit room. Her mother's

shape was outlined as she sat facing the window. Setting the tray down, she went to her. Even in the faint light, Tamara could tell her mother had been crying.

"I wish there was something I could do, Mom, but I don't know what." As both women stared out at the Christmas lights twinkling in the distant twilight, Tamara was at a loss for words, trying to make sense of what had gone on earlier that day.

"Well," Catherine said, breaking the silence, "now we know what your father was up to, and time will surely tell what Garrett is planning for us. But until then, there's no use worrying about it."

Catherine stood up and let out a big sigh.

Tamara moved to her mother and gently hugged her. As the embrace was broken, their eyes met, crystal blue and sparkling green, Tamara's heart ached when she saw the worry reflected in mother's eyes.

****

"So, you're saying that it happened on the bridge?" Michael tried not to sound too interested in what Nurse Palmer was saying as they drove back to the apartment.

"Yes, but you know, Michael, you really shouldn't have too much information about your donor. He's dead and you're alive, and that's the way the doctor wants to leave it."

"Okay." He let the subject drop, not wanting to raise any suspicions. But he had gotten what he had wanted, some concrete bits of information to get him started on his quest.

His donor was male. He had already suspected that from the images, but now he knew it to be fact. Secondly, the accident had happened right there in San Francisco. He could not believe his good fortune.

Hopefully, it would make his search a bit easier.

Without ever really coming out and saying it, Dr. Whitney had done his best to make Michael believe the donor had come from another area.

Nice move, Doctor Whitney, but hopefully not quite good enough.

"Excuse me, Nurse Palmer, would you mind if we made a quick stop at the library if it's still open? I'm all out of reading material and not having a computer or a TV is starting to get to me a little."

"Sure. No problem at all."

Michael looked out the window, trying to decide if the risk was worth it. Dr. Whitney's warnings played over and over in his head, but no matter how he approached the problem he always came to the same conclusion... *I made it through the operation, I am basically functional. Those two miracles alone should be enough proof that Dr. Whitney's theory is worth review and support. If what I am now choosing to do actually results in my death then that is where everyone can lay the blame. The failure of this experiment will rest squarely on my shoulders, because the risk to my life is worth attempting to save hers.*

Once inside the library Michael said, "I'm going to look through the shelves and see if there is anything in particular that interests me."

"All right. I'll wait over there"—Nurse Palmer pointed toward the back of the room—"and look through some magazines. Take all the time you want."

"Thanks," he said over his shoulder as he walked away, relieved that she seemed to be okay with waiting. He headed toward the tall rows of book shelves, keeping an eye on her. He watched as she selected a couple of magazines and made herself comfortable on one of the well-worn love seats in the reading area.

Damn, she had to choose a seat facing the computers. Why couldn't she have sat facing the other direction? This was not going to be as easy to pull off as he had thought. *Oh well, it doesn't matter; I'm here, and I'm going to take a shot at it anyway.*

Michael circled the entire perimeter of the massive book shelves. He stopped at the information desk and signed up to use the computer.

"Do you have a library card?" the girl at the counter asked without looking up at him.

"Uh, yes… yes, I believe I do."

"Card please."

"Mmmm, here." He fished out his old library card from his wallet, glancing back at Nurse Palmer as he handed it over.

The desk attendant looked up as she reached to take his card. "Thank you," she said, swiping his card.

Nervously, Michael rubbed the side of his nose with his finger, hoping this would not take too much longer.

"There, all done." She handed back his card. "You'll be on computer number three and your start time is in about five minutes."

"Okay, thank you."

"You're welcome," she mumbled back, already occupied with something else.

A young college student was just finishing up computer number three. Michael positioned himself so that Nurse Palmer couldn't see him as he waited for his turn.

The young man exited right on time and Michael

quickly took the seat. Looking back one more time, he could see Nurse Palmer had not moved an inch; her head was still bent down, fully engrossed in whatever she was reading.

Eyes closed, head down, heart pounding; *here goes*. He firmly pushed the 'on' button. Taking a deep breath, he opened his eyes and looked directly at the screen as it blinked to life. His fingers flew over the keyboard as he typed "fatal crash on the Golden Gate Bridge" and then the date into the search engine. Within seconds, he spotted what he was looking for. In big bold print it read, "Prominent Businessman Dies on Golden Gate Bridge."

Elated at his discovery, Michael looked over in the nurse's direction. He could tell she was getting restless as she started to shift positions. Convinced that this was what he was looking for, he took no time to read it. He pushed the copy button, turned off the computer, and grabbed the printed page as it emerged from the printer. Folding it in half, he decided he would read it as soon as he had some privacy.

Heading back to where the nurse was sitting, he realized he had not picked out any books. Passing a bookshelf, he grabbed the first two within his reach and turned toward the check-out desk. Spotting Nurse Palmer coming toward him, he hurriedly slipped the folded copy inside the top book. Then he randomly opened the book and scanned a few pages in case she were to ask him any questions on the subject.

"Well, did you find anything?"

"Yes, yes I did. And I was just on my way to check them out."

"May I see?"

"Sure," he replied, his heart pounding wildly as he handed them over to her.

"*Insects* and *Insects the Full Life Cycle*," she read out loud from the two book covers. She looked at him strangely. "I didn't think someone like you would be interested in insects."

"Oh, but I am," he said rolling his eyes at his lack of believable sincerity. "Have been ever since I was a kid." He cleared his throat. "You wouldn't believe how fascinating they are."

Nurse Palmer leafed through the books. Michael began to get nervous.

"Next please," an irritated voice said in their direction. They looked up slightly embarrassed.

Smiling, Nurse Palmer handed the books back to Michael.

"Why are you smiling?"

"Well, I guess it's true what they say."

"What's that?"

"That you learn something new every day."

Michael could only smile weakly at her, so relieved to have the books back in his possession.

****

By the time they returned to the apartment, Michael was truly exhausted.

"Why don't you go lie down awhile and I'll fix you something to eat."

"Okay," he said, heading to his bedroom, leaving his books on the kitchen table.

After fixing dinner, she went to get Michael. He was sound asleep. Deciding to let him sleep a little longer, she returned to the kitchen, sat down, and started browsing through one of the books Michael had checked out.

How could anyone be interested in this? Disgusted by the magnified photographs, she snapped the book shut, and as she did a folded piece of paper fell out. She opened it without even thinking. Reading the caption, she suddenly understood why Michael had been asking all those questions and wanted go to the library. She needed to contact Dr. Whitney right away.

Her instructions had been clear. She was to make sure that Michael ate dinner and took his anti-rejection medication before she left each evening, but this could not wait. Nurse Palmer quietly crept back to Michael's room. He was still asleep, but was beginning to stir, which, at this point, was not her main concern. What if Michael were to wake up and didn't follow through with his scheduled medication…well, she would just have to take that chance.

As Nurse Palmer left the apartment, her mind was screaming, *Oh My God. What have I done? How could I have been so lax? I've just threatened the entire experiment! Dr. Whitney is going to be so so angry with me.*

****

Michael squirmed in his bed. In the darkness, huge grotesque insects were crawling toward him. As they got closer, he twisted, trying to move out of their path. But it was no use. They continued forward until they were close enough to touch him. He swung, trying to smash them, but he could never make contact. When one finally crawled up onto his thigh, he was determined to get it. With deliberate calculation, he slowly lifted his hand as high as it could possibly go. The sheer force of the blow should crush the hideous creature. As his hand landed full force on his thigh, he knew he had made contact by the warm oozing liquid beneath it.

He looked down. The bug was flattened. He tried to brush it off his leg, but it wouldn't move. It wasn't real. It was a picture in a book. There were words underneath the picture.

"*Cockroach*: Any of an order (Blattaria) of chiefly nocturnal insects, including some that are domestic pests and with the recent..."

The words on the page blurred. Michael strained to read on.

"And with the recent information you have provided me, this anticipated confusion will make it most convenient for me to complete our agreement as planned."

I won't be leaving, *he thought as he folded the piece of paper, returned it to the envelope, and placed it into the black box. He locked the box and put the box back in the bottom drawer. The sound of shattering glass was piercing. Shimmering pieces were falling all around him. The sound of someone's hysterical laughter filled the room. No, it couldn't be him...*but it was.

He couldn't believe that the hideous sound was coming from his own throat. The nightmare was beyond what a normal, rational mind could tolerate and still remain sane. It had to stop. He had to stop it now!

He was determined not to lose this battle; if he did he might never be the same. Keeping his eyes closed he waited. Soon his mind resumed a steady flow of congruent thoughts and memories. He forced his mind to separate small fragments of memories and images that he was absolutely sure belonged to him.

Slowly, all that were left were the unfamiliar images, and as they began to fade, one last ominous image passed through his mind. *"Well, Catherine, my dear, that's exactly what is going to happen to you,"* he said, as he viewed the damaged picture.

That solitary image lodged in Michael's mind was as vivid as a neon sign flashing in total darkness. He lay there knowing he was fully awake. He could no longer explain away what he had just experienced as a bad dream. He was afraid to relax and let his mind wander yet realized he would be unable to control his thoughts forever. He was just not ready to have these bizarre images repeat themselves.

Time and exhaustion finally won the struggle. Michael's resolve to have total control over his thoughts weakened and he started to relax. Nothing resembling the disturbing images surfaced, just random thoughts and pictures that he recognized. Michael again closed his eyes. Suddenly, a piece of crucial information flashed in his mind.

Catherine.

He had called her Catherine. The name passed through his mind again. *Her name was Catherine!* He now had a name to go with those incredible blue eyes.

Chapter 23

Stephanie stood under the warm spray of water, her shoulders curled forward. Ordinarily she would find it to be soothing, but not this time. Every part of her body ached. She turned slowly until she faced the gentle stream. She raised her bruised and swollen face to meet the spray of pain-inducing drops. Each time the water touched her face, she could taste the fresh blood as it flowed from the split in her lip.

The night before had been like a nightmare. Garrett had stormed into her apartment, quite obviously having been drinking heavily.

He started ranting and raving, yelling and flinging every insult he could think of at her. He was so drunk, Stephanie could not make out much of what he was saying, but that did not seem to matter to him.

He continued to hurl horrible, biting obscenities at her. At first she did not respond, not quite knowing what to do. This only seemed to infuriate him more. Then he began to hit her. She could hear her own screams. Every scream was met with a twisted smile and a renewed bout of indescribable savagery. As the beating continued, Stephanie knew she was powerless and could do no more than scream in hopes that someone might hear her. But the more she screamed and begged him to stop, the wilder he became. It was if her cries of pain gave him pleasure and spurred him on.

Blow after blow was delivered as his tirade continued.

Finally, after what had seemed like hours, Stephanie's body had taken all it was physically capable of, and graciously released her from consciousness.

****

When he awoke, he remembered the article he had hidden in the library book. He could not wait to read it. He hastened to the kitchen. The book was on the kitchen table, right where he had left it.

He picked it up and flipped through the pages. He shook the book so that the pages hung free, but nothing fell out. It wasn't there. The article was gone. Michael searched the apartment. He went down and checked where the car had been parked. He retraced every step he had taken from the car to his apartment, but the copy was simply not there.

After doubling checking every place he had been, he resigned himself to the fact that it must have slipped out somewhere between the library and getting into the car.

"Damn. I wish I had taken the time to read it." To search any more would be a waste of time. *I'll just have to go back to the library and get another copy*, he decided as he hurriedly showered and dressed. Strapping his watch around his wrist, he checked the time.

"But there is one small problem." He chided his own stupidity. *It's only six o'clock in the morning and the library doesn't open until nine. It's going to be three very long hours.*

Now there was nothing left to do but wait. He put on a pot of coffee and watched as it brewed. This wasn't getting him anywhere. He went to the living room and took a pen and a notepad from his briefcase. He'd make a list of everything he knew so far. Hopefully, that would help clarify things.

Back in the kitchen, he poured himself a cup of coffee and moved to the table. He sat back in the chair with the steaming coffee held tightly in his hand, letting his mind run through the information he currently had.

He's a man.

He lived right here in San Francisco…well, maybe not. He could have been a tourist…no, I don't think so.

He died on the Golden Gate Bridge, about the same day and time I lost consciousness. This is a fact.

They both ended up at the same hospital. Michael was pretty secure that this was also fact. It would have been too complicated to transport the delicate tissue, complete the intricate operation, and maintain the strict veil of secrecy without every little detail planned out and pre-arranged ahead of time.

The timing was absolutely perfect. Lucky for me, not so lucky for him. Realizing the astronomical odds for this to have happened, Michael was astounded. Intense emotions welled up inside of him, emotions he didn't know he still had.

He stopped and took a big swallow of the strong dark liquid and tried to get his thoughts back on track. He believed he was getting closer…but closer to what? He still didn't have any concrete answers.

He got up, stretched, and paced about the small kitchen. Feeling better, he sat back down and continued with his list. *He is a bigwig in some major corporation.* He scribbled after this note, "name of corporation, unknown."

A beautiful woman…she is, or was, blonde…with crystal blue eyes. She is tied to his life somehow. Closely tied, recalling the intensity of the emotions he had experienced when she appeared. *She has made him angry. Angry enough to harm her and her name is…* Michael paused, straining to recall her name. It was there in the back of his mind. *Her name is…is…Catherine! Catherine. Yes, that's it! And he is going to…he is going to…what?*

His mind would go no further. Whatever "he" had planned for Catherine certainly did not exist in Michael's current thought processes, and the only way to finish out this image was to deliberately bring it on. He wasn't sure he wanted to, but it had to be done in order to move forward.

Reluctantly, he closed his eyes, cleared his mind, and soon the beautiful blonde image stood before him. His body immediately filled with an intense loathing as he stared directly into those icy blue eyes. Their eyes were locked in silent hatred. *I am going to kill you.* Michael's eyes flew open. The declaration had been issued as a statement of fact, not as a mere empty threat. Most shocking of all was that Michael knew it had been issued directly from him.

He panicked. He didn't know what to do with this new image. Michael knew himself well enough to know that he was incapable of killing anyone.

Michael remained motionless in the chair, trying to relax. Even in the reassuring stillness of his own kitchen, he found it hard to grasp what had just happened and what he could possibly do to stop it.

I know I'm missing something. He read his list over and over, searching for answers. There was something he wasn't picking up on, but what was it?

Suddenly it dawned on him.

"That's it! That's it!" he repeated, suddenly elated. "He can't kill her...he's already dead!" Michael's body flooded with relief. But as soon as he began to feel better, a sense of defeat invaded him with a new realization.

No, of course he couldn't kill her...but he could have arranged to have her killed. *And somehow, I've become a part of the arrangement?*

"God, I don't believe this." He got up from the chair and paced back and forth.

"But how is it going to happen?" The information had to be somewhere inside of him. *"But how?"* He repeated this question several more times to himself, rapidly trying to search through the information he had stored in his mind. Suddenly, he hit upon something that he'd seen earlier, but hadn't recognized it as relevant.

The letter. What about the letter in the black box? It could hold some kind of an answer. He remembered the feeling of being in total control as he watched the letter being secured in the black box and placed back in the drawer. It had to be important. Here was another piece to add to the already confusing puzzle.

Michael was certain the images were not random thoughts, nor were they connected to events that had previously happened. That was just not possible. The answer was out there somewhere. He just needed to focus.

What if I take control of the images?

The more he thought about it, the more he believed his driving the images forward might work. With renewed conviction, he sat perfectly still and forced himself to systematically pull up each individual image. As they played through his mind he tried to focus on every little detail.

Slowly, Michael began to grasp the connection. He was right. These weren't random thoughts or repressed emotions as the doctor suggested. They were actual memories. Somehow, Dr. Whitney's procedure had dropped him right in the middle of his donor's murder plan.

"Oh my god. There's no way." But it was the only answer that made any sense and seemed to connect the pictures that had plagued him for so long. He was now more than convinced the attempt was going to take place in the future.

He knew what he had to do and knew that he would do it with or without the consent of Dr. Whitney. He had no choice. If he didn't try to stop it, someone was going to die. He could not live with himself knowing that he was a part of a life-threatening scheme, unwilling or not, and did nothing to try to prevent it.

"Damn," he said, feeling frustrated. *I wish I had that article. I would at least know who he was, which might help me find out who she is and how I could possibly track her down.* No matter how difficult it proved to be, he would follow through with it.

His mind pitched one unanswered question after another. *What's going to happen when I do find her? How will I ever be able to explain this unique situation to her? Will she even listen to a complete stranger? I wouldn't, so why should she? And if by chance I do get past all of these hurdles, and she does listen, how can I get her to believe me without coming across like a total maniac?* It seemed like an insurmountable task.

He looked at the clock…an hour and a half still to go. He was getting impatient. He needed to get that article, yet there was another source of information that would be even more valuable, if only he would cooperate.

I'm going to stop by Dr. Whitney's office one more time. With all that's gone on, I might be able to convince him to tell me what I need.

Michael knew his attempt would be a long shot. It would also increase the strain on their already tense relationship, but this was too important. He had to take that risk.

Maybe, just maybe, if I can convince him I can do this without jeopardizing his work, he'll agree to help me. Hopeful, he gulped down the last of the coffee.

A couple of answers are all I need, and I'm positive it will make finding this Catherine so much easier. Michael walked out the front door, got into his car and headed for Dr. Whitney's office. He was a so preoccupied with what he needed to do, it never dawned on him it was the first time he had driven in months.

Chapter 24

"Hello, I'd like to speak with Mrs. Paxton, please." She tried to keep the nervousness out of her voice.

"Who's calling, please?"

"Uhmm, Stephanie. Stephanie Delaney," she answered, knowing that by giving her true name she could encounter a flat refusal.

"Hold on, Miss Delaney. I'll see if she's in."

There was silence on the other end of the line, but within seconds a cool voice responded. "Yes, Miss Delaney, what can I do for you?"

"Is this Mrs. Paxton?" She knew the answer before she even asked the question.

"Yes, it is."

God, she was so nervous. She cleared her throat. "Mrs. Paxton... I'm calling to let you know that I've sent a certified letter to Mr. White stating I am not now, nor will I ever be requesting any sort of monetary compensation as the listed beneficiary or for my silence in all matters pertaining to Scottford Textiles." She continued on quickly, not even pausing to take a breath. "Any information I have that could do any possible harm to you or your family will remain with me."

But there was no response from the other end of the line. "Did you hear me, Mrs. Paxton?"

"Yes, I did, but I'm not quite sure I understand exactly why you're doing this?"

Stephanie closed her eyes. She thought she wouldn't need an explanation, but apparently she did. Mrs. Paxton was not going to let her off the hook that easily.

"Well…what I mean is… I really loved your son and I wanted to see him happy and.. and…" Stephanie was getting flustered. "And it was all a terrible, terrible mistake!" She started to cry. *Damn, I wasn't going to do this!*

"I am already aware of your connection to my son," Catherine said. "And if it helps any I can actually understand how this could have happened."

Hearing some compassion in Catherine's voice, Stephanie believed she had an obligation to this extraordinary woman to let her know what an emotional tightrope her son was walking. Maybe, in some small way, this could help offset some of the damage she had done.

"Mrs. Paxton, I feel I need to let you know…" She stopped, not knowing how to word what she knew she had to say.

"Yes, Miss Delaney?"

"Garrett… Garrett has some very serious psychological problems. You need to help him before it's too late." There, she had said it. She sincerely hoped that bringing it out in the open would help him. This ended her commitment to Garrett. She was now totally free to move on.

A barely audible, "I know," was all the stunned Stephanie received from the other end. The complete resignation and defeat in those two words told her everything.

Quietly, she said, "I'm sorry. So, very very sorry."

****

After hearing the soft click of the receiver being placed back in its cradle, Catherine sat back in the chair. Something serious had happened, something bad enough to scare this woman into walking away from a small fortune. Both women were aware there were millions in play. So why had she given it all up? What had happened to make her change her mind? And where was Garrett now?

Catherine picked up the phone and dialed Garrett's number, but after the fourth ring she hung up. He was either not at home or not answering. Her motherly instinct gave her a sense of urgency. She needed to know if he was all right. Realizing none of the hideous things that Garrett had said or done could be changed, her desire to help her son was as strong as ever. Her concern for him always outweighed the pain he caused her.

She picked up the phone again and made a call. At the end of her conversation, she felt somewhat relieved that she would have some answers.

About an hour later, the phone rang and Catherine answered, not having moved from the chair. Unfortunately, her caller had little success in locating her son. Garrett had not been seen at his apartment for the last few days. None of the neighbors had any idea where he had gone. The investigator apologized for having so little information but assured her that he would continue looking until he located Garrett.

How much more could happen? With Stephanie walking away from everything, the company's stability was no longer in question, but Garrett's emotional stability was.

All she could do was wait until he surfaced. Inwardly she said a little prayer, hoping that would be enough to protect her son. Sadly, it would take a great deal more than her prayers to protect Garrett from himself.

Chapter 25

"All right, Dr. Whitney, I know we have an agreement, but I have to know who my donor is!" The desperation in Michael's voice was palpable.

"He's planning to have her killed! Did you hear what I said? Killed! And I honestly believe I can do something to stop it from happening."

Dr. Whitney made no attempt to answer him. He sat quietly in his chair as Michael continued.

"Please, tell me who he is. Tell me something… anything will help!"

"Calm down, Michael, I know this is important to you, but I can't give you that information. We spoke about this at great length, and you agreed that total confidentiality surrounding every aspect of the operation was of the utmost importance no matter the circumstances."

"I know I did. But with what I know now, doesn't it sort of change everything?"

"It doesn't for me. Even if you are truly convinced, which I am not, that you could change the outcome and could do so without any type of exposure, I still can't help you."

Michael couldn't hide his disappointment.

"Michael you've got to understand that after all the years of work I have put into this, I'm not willing to take even the smallest amount of risk, no matter what the situation is."

"Okay then, answer me this, Doctor. Is that why Nurse Palmer took the newspaper article, knowing that I was trying to track down my donor? Maybe I was getting a little too close for comfort?" Michael didn't like the tone he was using, but he couldn't help himself.

"Yes, that's why she took it. She was very upset when she informed me what you were doing and the risks you took in doing so."

"But look at me! I'm fine. I'm living proof that it works!" He turned full circle as he said it.

"Michael, please don't get involved." Dr. Whitney looked worried.

"I have to, you know I do."

A heavy silence hovered between the two men. Dr. Whitney shook his head and looked down. "I believe you'll be risking everything for nothing," he murmured.

"That could be, but I can't just sit back and let this happen."

"I know, but I can't help you either. I'm sorry."

****

"I'm sorry, sir, our computers are all down for servicing."

"They were all working yesterday."

"Well, we had a power surge about fifteen minutes ago and our server crashed. Let me call the other branches to see any of theirs are up and running."

As Michael stood at the counter, he could feel himself losing patience.

"Well, this is odd," the librarian said, returning to the counter. "None of the other branches have internet access either."

Michael smiled. *My, my, Dr. Whitney, you do have*

friends in high places, don't you?

"Thank you. I appreciate you taking the time to make some calls for me."

"You're welcome."

Michael headed straight to the pay phone in the lobby and dialed the private line.

"Dr. Whitney?"

"Yes?"

"One more question."

"Go ahead."

"Should I waste my time going across town to…let's say…the newspaper office?"

"I wouldn't."

"Okay, thanks." He hung up and took a deep breath. *This is going to be a lot harder than I thought.* He walked out of the library and straight into the rain.

"Damn it," he said under his breath, running toward his car. By the time he arrived home, it was pouring. Luckily, he found a parking space close to the building. It was the only thing that had gone right for him today.

His lucky streak was short lived. When he reached the front of his apartment, he found the newspaper had been tossed onto the stairs, not quite making it to the stoop. It was soaking wet.

"I don't believe this," he muttered, grabbing the mushy paper and letting himself in.

Michael took the wet paper into the kitchen and carefully unfolded it. It was soaked completely through. He separated the pages, draping each section on the back of a chair to dry.

Hanging the last piece, a photograph caught his eye. He picked it up, staring. He couldn't believe what he was seeing. It was her. Her face was slightly turned away and she was standing beside someone who was totally shielded, but it was her! He read and then reread the article, even in black and white he found himself staring at those familiar eyes. So this was Catherine. Catherine Scottford Paxton.

Chapter 26

He sat at the bar hunched over his drink. The Christmas lights twinkled around the long mirror behind the dark mahogany bar. It was a feeble attempt to create the Christmas spirit. A couple of the girls had attempted to be festive, dressing in red or green and donning cheesy red Santa hats set on an angle atop their mounds of teased-up hair.

Garrett's head was bursting with ugly scenes. Over and over they played in his mind. The picture of his mother's blue eyes with so much pain in them—pain he knew he had put there—haunted him.

Then there was auburn hair flying in all directions as he repeatedly yanked Stephanie up off the floor, hitting the soft white flesh. Her weak protests only made him laugh.

The bitch. She deserved everything she got. How dare she try to back out on me now.

Over the phone Stephanie had told him that she wanted no part in helping him destroy his family. She was done.

By the time Garrett reached her apartment, he was so infuriated that nothing Stephanie said or did could stop him. Only when her body went limp in his hands did his savage tirade subside.

"I don't need you...you bitch!" he'd yelled, throwing her motionless body against the wall. Her head hit with a thud. A spattering of bright red spots appeared on the cream colored wall.

He surveyed the damage he had done, his eyes finally taking in the bloodied wall and her battered body on the floor. He stood motionless, making no attempt to come to Stephanie's aid. Abruptly, he turned and walked out of the apartment without a backward glance. That was the last thing he could remember.

Garrett finished his drink. "Hey," he yelled at the bartender, lifting his hand with the empty glass to catch his attention.

"Another?"

"Yeah." Garrett bobbed his head.

The bartender singled one of the girls with a sideway nod in Garrett's direction.

"Hi, sweetie," she purred in his ear.

Garrett did not respond, but he could smell the sickening sweetness of her cheap perfume.

"You look like you could use a little company." She positioned her voluptuous body close to his.

Garrett still did not respond, his head remaining in a downward tilt. She glanced over at the bartender, who was pouring Garrett another drink. She paused as if she wasn't sure what to do next. The bartender took the lead.

"Hey," he said loudly, "this is my friend Chrissy. She'd like to spend some time with you. Would ya like that?"

Garrett slowly raised his head. His eyes traveled up an ample bust that had been stuffed into a rather ill-fitting bustier. As his gaze continued, he was pleasantly surprised at the round girlish face so close to his own.

How old was she? It didn't matter. He knew why

she was being so friendly. He looked lecherously at her full pink lips. *God, what would those feel like?*

"Yeah, I want to spend some time with her," he slurred and pulled a wad of bills from his pocket. He peeled the first two off the top and put them on the counter. The bartender looked down at the money, two hundred dollars bills. He swiftly scooped it up, looking around to see if anyone had seen him.

"Well, mister, Chrissy is gonna be real good to you. Won't you, Chrissy?"

"Yeah, real good to you," she said in a throaty voice, placing his hand inside the tight lace covering her breasts. "Come on, sweetie. Why don't we go someplace where we can make ourselves more comfortable?" She gently pulled him off the tall stool, leading him through a set of beaded curtains and up the back stairs to one of the small rooms.

Garrett didn't notice a nondescript man sitting at a small table intently watching the action at the bar. After he disappeared from view, the man paid his bill, tipped the waitress, and headed out the front door.

****

Michael was so excited, he could hardly contain himself. Just when he thought his search was hopeless, her picture popped out at him.

"Okay, Michael ol' boy," he said to himself, "now that you know who she is, what are you going to do about it? And let's be logical about it," he continued talking out loud. "Number one, you have to figure out how to contact her. Number two, you have to convince her to listen to you. And the hardest of all, is number three, trying to do this without coming across like some nut job or an escapee from a mental institution." He sat down, trying to pull himself together. He needed to come up with a solid plan of action. After constructing several different scenarios and finding a major flaw in each, he shoved himself back from the table, exasperated.

How can I do this and keep my promise to Dr. Whitney? He shook his head at the seemingly impossible task. If there was a way, he knew he would find it. But it would not be tonight. He'd gotten so engrossed in his dilemma that he lost track of time. It was four-thirty in the morning. Realizing he wouldn't accomplish anything at that late hour, he headed to bed.

Before he fell asleep, he came to at least one firm decision. The next day he would take a little drive downtown and have a look at the Scottford Textiles Corporation.

Chapter 27

Catherine and Tamara sat together in the spacious living room, both admiring the elegant Christmas tree the staff had put up for them. Yet, neither mother nor daughter were in the mood for their yearly ritual.

Tamara was the first to speak. "Mom…why don't we skip this for now?"

Catherine's face brightened. "Sounds like a good idea to me." She stood up, took Tamara by the arm, and headed straight for the kitchen, neither of them taking a second look at the mounds of unopened gifts beneath the beautiful tree.

****

It was Michael's third time around the block. The magnificent steel and glass building reached high above the natural skyline, dwarfing the surrounding buildings. Looking at it made him wonder if getting involved was such a good idea. It would be so much easier on everyone just to leave things alone—at least it would be for him—but he couldn't do that, especially now that he had a face with a name.

The traffic was light as he sat at the stop sign on the corner. Most people were at home or with relatives, enjoying the holiday. Michael was in no hurry to get home. He had no one to celebrate with.

When he finally decided to turn the corner, he knew his life had taken a turn, too. He would contact

Catherine Paxton. He would do whatever it took to convince her that a series of events had already begun and he believed…no, he knew, would prove fatal unless something was done to change them.

He still did not know how he was going to do it, but he would have to find a way to make her listen to him. Any indecision he had been feeling was now gone. He was ready to take on this seemingly impossible task, no matter what he might encounter.

Driving back to his apartment, Michael realized how incredible all this would sound to Mrs. Paxton, because it sounded incredible to him. But he wouldn't allow any amount of doubt to sway him. It had to be done. His decision was made. There was no turning back. He had nothing to turn back to anyway, and he could not live with himself if he did.

****

"Hello, Mrs. Paxton, sorry to bother you on the holiday and everything."

"It's no bother, really. Did you find out anything?"

"Yes, I found him. I located him at Tassels." He sounded embarrassed.

"Tassels?"

"Yes, ma'am. It's a strip joint over on Broadway."

"Oh, I see. Is he all right?" Her concern over-shadowed her discomfort.

"He appeared to be all right. He was drunk and in the company of a young lady of…of questionable…"

"I understand," she cut in, knowing what he was trying to say. "Thank you, Detective. Please let me know if anything changes."

"I sure will, ma'am."

"And Detective, I really do mean it when I say

thank you."

"No problem, ma'am. Goodbye."

"Goodbye," she said softly.

****

"Merry Christmas," she squealed into his ear while tickling his ribs.

"What? What the hell are you talking about?" he groaned, shoving her away. Garrett rolled over onto his back. He squinted as the daylight hit him in the face.

"It's Christmas," she said meekly.

Garrett shielded his eyes from the brightness. A naked body was perched beside him on the bed. He looked at her face. Her lips were formed into a slight pout.

Those lips; God, those lips! Just looking at them gave him an erection.

"Let's do something special," she said, trying to divert him, but it was too late.

"Oh, honey, I intend to," he responded in a throaty voice. He reached up and grabbed her by the hair, entwining his fingers to have total control of her head.

"Owww, you're hurting me." Her voice rose. "Don't!" she yelled and began struggling. "Let go. Please!"

He laughed at her as he forced her head down. She tried to pull up, but he held tight until she conceded to his wishes.

"Oh baby," he moaned as she skillfully slid her lips over him. "This is special. This is real special."

Chapter 28

By the time Michael returned to the apartment, he was both physically and mentally exhausted. Walking into the sparse living room he immediately noticed a small flat screen television sitting on a stand with a bow and a note taped to it. Curious, he walked over and opened the note.

Michael,

If turning on a computer did no harm, neither should this.

Merry Christmas,

Dr. Whitney

Michael smiled at the peace offering. Forgetting how tired he was, he picked up the remote and began channel surfing. Hours later and the grumbling of his stomach signaled Michael he also hadn't eaten. Heading back from the kitchen with a sandwich he picked up the newspaper he had spread out earlier to dry. He sat down on the couch and reread the article in which Catherine appeared.

She was such a beautiful woman. *Why would anyone want to harm her?* It did not make much sense to him. *How am I ever going to warn her of something that is going to happen when I don't even have enough information to tell her what that something is?*

Feeling tired again, Michael closed his eyes. He heard voices mingled with laughter. Somewhere in the distance, he heard soft music, the old-fashioned kind that makes you want to take someone in your arms and glide across the dance floor.

Michael was not asleep, but if he opened his eyes the image would disappear. So with skillful deliberation, he relaxed his body and let the images begin progress on their own.

He could see her. She was right in front of him. Her blue eyes were unusually bright. She was…he could not explain what he was seeing. The only word that could remotely describe the image was shimmering. She was shimmering.

Michael looked around trying to figure out where he was, but everything surrounding him was illuminated and gave off the same type of luminous glow. He turned back in her direction, but she was gone. He stood alone in a maze of color.

The voices got louder. The laughter now held an edge of anticipated excitement, yet he could not see anything beyond the wall of color. Something drew his attention up. Above him was the beautiful night sky, filled with glittering stars.

The music struck a chord of announcement. Within seconds the sky appeared to part and the same illuminating colors that had surrounded him fell from above. There were screams of delight as the laughter reached a fevered pitch.

The colors from above drifted downward and were now close enough to touch. Michael felt like he was suffocating. Despite desperately wanting to see this one through to its entirety, he could no longer keep himself immersed in the chaotic scene. Whatever was happening was important, but the pressure in his chest became unbearable. Gasping for breath, he opened his eyes and the images immediately disappeared. All that was left was the wild beating of his heart and a huge sense of failure.

****

As he had promised himself, Michael's first stop the following morning was the Scottford Textiles Corporation Building. Even though it was his second visit, it was no less intimidating.

He stood on the sidewalk and looked up at the tall structure. Again he questioned his reasons for coming here. But after the intensity of the previous night's image, he knew whatever was going to happen was going to happen soon.

Taking a deep breath, he walked inside the lobby. It was exquisite. The gray and white marble floors shone as if no one ever walked on them. He took in everything around him, including the manned security booth located back by the elevators.

Quickly he made some mental calculations and headed back out onto the street, hopefully without calling any attention to himself. He was nervous, much more so than he thought he would be by simply walking through the building.

When he reached his car, he turned and looked back and as he did so he observed a small blonde woman enter the building. The hairs on the back of his neck stood on end. He involuntarily jerked forward, as if a high volt of electricity had been shot through his entire body.

There was a loud ringing in his ears. He threw his hands up to cover them in an ineffective attempt to stop the noise. The ringing was getting louder and louder. It was deafening.

He had to do something. With great difficulty, he got himself into the car and was able to close the door behind him. His head was pounding with pain, seeming to coincide with the ringing. The louder the sound, the stronger the pain.

I'm going to die. I'm going to die. This was not a smart move on my part. Michael's mind screamed as the pain escalated.

Michael rocked his body back and forth. He had no idea how long he rocked, but eventually the ringing and throbbing subsided and the rocking motion slowed until he was sitting motionless. His hands were still tightly clasped over his ears, fearing that the slightest movement would cause the pain to reoccur.

His arms were stiff. Unaware of how long he had been in this position, the tightness in his muscles told him it had been for quite some time. He removed his hands from over his ears, lowered them slowly and began rubbing his aching forearms. It was time to get out of there, he fumbled trying to get his keys into the ignition. Executing extreme caution, he started the engine and pulled out onto the street. Drenched in perspiration and still shaking, Michael headed home.

Chapter 29

"Good morning, Mrs. Paxton," the security guard said as she passed the booth.

"Good morning, Ben." She returned his greeting, smiling.

When she reached the penthouse, she was again greeted with regard as she inquired if her daughter was in her office.

"Yes, she is, Mrs. Paxton," replied Grace. "She said to have you go directly in."

Catherine walked through the doors into the spacious office.

"Hi, Mom." Tamara greeted her without even looking up from the reports she was reading. "I'm almost finished."

Catherine watched her daughter with pride. With Tamara's head bent, the sun reflected off the golden highlights in her blonde hair. Her reading glasses had slipped to the end of her small nose as she read with such a serious expression, "No hurry. Our appointment isn't until eleven."

Seeing her daughter like this, Catherine was satisfied that she had made the right decision in letting Tamara take over the majority of the business. The corporation was in extremely capable hands.

"There." Tamara stood up and came from behind the desk, picked up her purse and in one swift motion took her mother by the arm and headed out the door.

"Grace, I'll be back by two," she announced as she and Catherine passed by the secretary's desk.

"All right, Miss Paxton."

Arm and arm, the two women disappeared from view.

****

"Honey, go downstairs and get us another bottle," Garrett commanded, viewing the empty Jack Daniels bottle on the night stand.

"But I ain't got no money, sweetie," she said, trying to sound innocent.

"Shit. Do I have to do everything?" he mumbled, making a feeble attempt to get up off the bed.

"Here, sweetie." Chrissy rushed over and placed both palms on his chest, rubbing her breasts against him as she gently pushed him back onto the pillows.

"Tell me what you want and I'll go get it for you," she whispered seductively, darting the tip of her tongue into his ear, then moving down to his earlobe.

"Okay, okay," he said, amused as she nibbled on his neck. "There's some money in my pants, in the pockets. Get a couple of twenties and go get a bottle."

"Be glad to," she replied, rubbing her sensuous body against him again.

He started to grab her, but this time she saw it coming and quickly moved out of his reach.

"Now don't you move," she instructed as she bent over his rumpled pants hastily discarded on the floor a few days prior.

Garrett was easily distracted with a good view of her long, lean legs and her well rounded buttocks as she fished through his pockets. Without detection Chrissy slipped a couple of hundred dollar bills in her garter then she held up two twenty-dollar bills for his inspection.

"Here, I found some."

"Let's forget about the bottle for now, and you can come right back here," he said patting the bed.

"Sweetie, you hold that place for me. This will only take a minute." She slipped on a sheer kimono and headed out to get rid of the money. "I'll be right back, with a brand new bottle for us," she called out.

"Shit. Bitch, you better hurry back," he yelled as the door closed behind her.

Chapter 30

"Are you ready?" Tamara called out.

"Ready!" Catherine answered.

On cue, both women emerged from the heavily curtained dressing rooms and simultaneously stepped in front of the three-sided full-length mirror that stood between the two rooms.

All movement in the room ceased. Everyone stared in awe at the reflection revealed in the massive mirror, including the two who caused this extraordinary illusion. They looked almost identical.

"Unbelievable," one of the designer's assistants said under her breath.

Mother and daughter looked into the mirror, then at each other. The effect was incredible.

Tamara was ecstatic. "This is exactly what I had in mind. We didn't know how it would be done, but if anyone could do it, you could! Thank you so much, Madame Russo," she bubbled excitedly. Tamara twirled in front of the mirror, her gown sparkled, catching the light as she did so. "Trying them on together, we really do look like the zodiac sign, Gemini!"

"Yes, thank you, Madame Russo. The gowns are absolutely gorgeous. I really don't know how you were able to fix mine with so many of the crystals crushed and the horrific tears in the delicate material. I really thought it had been ruined beyond repair. You truly are a miracle worker," Catherine added, sharing in her daughter's delight.

Madame Russo blushed under the generous compliments. "Now hold still, hold still," she fussed, as her oversized body bustled about them, making notes about each dress.

The two women stood perfectly still in their exquisite teal gowns. The dresses hugged their bodies flawlessly. Row upon row of blueish-green crystals had been hand sewn into place, giving off an iridescent glow each time they moved.

On their heads, a cap of the same hand-beaded material held their blonde hair snugly underneath. Long strands of the same sparkling crystals dangled creating a frame around their faces.

The resemblance was uncanny, almost unnerving. The only noticeable difference between them was the color of their eyes.

"All right, ladies." Madame Russo clapped her hands, ordering her assistants back to work. Quickly each worker went over all the beading, checking every seam and making sure even the slightest bit of alteration was noted to ensure the proper fit.

By the time the whole process was completed, Catherine and Tamara were glad to get back into their own clothes.

"I'm starving," Tamara declared.

"Where would you like to go?"

"How about Rikki's?"

"Sounds good to me."

As they headed for the door, a scowl of reproach was aimed in their direction. Madame Russo was standing with her arm crossed in disapproval.

"What is it?" Catherine asked.

"You eat too much, you spoil the dress," she said in her broken English, trying to hide her smile.

They laughed at her attempt to scold them. "Don't worry, we won't," Catherine said.

Tamara went right over and hugged the old woman, who responded by shooing her away, laughing as she did. "As much as I like to eat, I wouldn't dare eat my way out of that beautiful gown," she teased, cooing to her as if to a small child. Madame Russo laughed at Tamara's playfulness.

"Ready, Mom?" She turned toward her mother.

"Yes, I'm ready."

"Thank you again, Madame Russo," Catherine said, laughing as she, too, got caught up in her daughter's antics.

"Go, go. Enough of this silliness. Go eat your lunch." She waved them toward the front door.

"Yes, we're leaving." Tamara gave her a little pout, but then replaced it with a genuine smile of deep appreciation. Opening the front door, Madame Russo returned the smile, and the two women were on their way.

****

"Well, Michael, everything checks out okay," Dr. Whitney said, completing his physical examination. "I believe this episode was a severe anxiety attack." He watched to see how Michael reacted to that statement. Michael did not respond.

"Physically, you are fine. But honestly I'm now a little worried about your mental health."

"You don't have to be."

"But I am."

"I'll be all right."

"I know you will, but that's not the point." Dr. Whitney took a deep breath and continued. "I realize this is extremely hard on you and I'm not providing all the answers you need."

"I understand, I do."

"But, if there's anything else I can help you with, please let me know." The words were barely out of the doctor's mouth when he realized he should not have made the offer.

"Yes, since you offered, I need you to explain the situation and verify that what I'm saying is indeed possible. Just to her. No one else needs to know."

"I'm sorry, Michael. I can't do that."

"Are you sure there's no possible way, under any circumstances, you would feel comfortable disclosing just some of the information to protect her?"

"Unfortunately, I'm sure."

"Okay, okay." Michael put up his hands in resignation. He got down from the examining table and dressed. Neither man spoke.

"Dr. Whitney, you know, with or without your help, I'm going to do something."

"I know." With a show of acceptance and avoiding any further discussion, Dr. Whitney stuck out his hand to the younger man. Michael accepted it with a firm shake. "Please let Nurse Palmer return with you in case you should have another attack."

"No thank you, Doctor. I need to take care of this on my own."

****

Dr. Whitney truly understood Michael's anger and his compelling need to act upon what he believed to be true. It was admirable. Hadn't he handpicked Michael for those exact same ethical qualities he was now exhibiting? *Am I asking too much of this man...or possibly of any man?*

Chapter 31

Rikki's was crowded, as always. Once seated and served, Tamara ate heartily.

"I don't know how you do it." Catherine watched her daughter in amazement.

"What? Oh, this?" She pointed at her almost empty plate. "I don't know. Lucky I guess." She shrugged and smiled at her mother.

Catherine had to keep an eye on everything she ate, while Tamara, like the old saying goes, could eat like a horse. She could eat anything and never gain a pound. She must have inherited that particular gene from her father, Catherine decided.

Having satisfied her appetite, Tamara asked, "Mom, have you heard any more about Garrett?"

"No, nothing new." Catherine veiled her emotions carefully. "I'm sure as soon as there is something Detective Costanza will let me know."

"Well, I'm glad Miss Delaney was smart enough to get out while she was still ahead!" Tamara said vehemently.

"I understand how you feel, honey, but remember, if Miss Delaney hadn't backed out as gracefully as she did, it would have taken months, maybe even years to repair the damage that kind of publicity would have caused the company."

Catherine could see the anger reflected in her

daughter's eyes.

"You know, Mr. White has done an excellent job of squelching any rumors that surfaced about your father, his affair, and his overall questionable ethics when it came to company dealings. He really has gone above and beyond to get everything back in order."

"Yes, but…"

"Tamara, having our personal affairs in the headlines, even for a couple of days, was hard, just think how hard it would be if *everything* became public. I think we've been through the worst of it, and we're okay. Aren't we?" Catherine looked questioningly into her daughter's eyes.

"I guess we are." She reluctantly agreed and took her mother's hand, squeezing it.

Catherine smiled at her beautiful daughter. She had been through so much in such a short amount of time. She had every right to be angry and resentful, as long as she didn't hold on to those feelings forever.

Catherine was all too aware of what could happen if you didn't move on in life. This was where Garrett had gotten stuck; he had never moved on. *Poor Garrett, I wonder what he's doing now?*

"Mom, I have a few errands to run before I return to the office, so I'd better get going," Tamara said, breaking into Catherine's thoughts. She leaned over to kiss her mother goodbye.

"Okay, sweetie."

Tamara started to exit the restaurant, but turned back. "Mom?"

"Yes?" Catherine looked up from her cup of tea.

"I love you."

"Love you, too."

****

Michael was discouraged. Unsuccessful at getting any cooperation from the doctor, he decided to spend the rest of the afternoon figuring out a way to make contact with Catherine. There had to be a way.

This was not going to be easy. How could he just walk right up and convince someone that they were in danger, especially someone of Catherine Paxton's stature?

Michael envisioned the disastrous scene. There he is, trying to explain to her that even though she doesn't know him, he knows she is in danger. Her natural response to something as bizarre as this would certainly be to seek someone out to protect her and he really couldn't blame her.

He pictured himself following her, trying to finish his explanation. But before he could persuade her to stop and listen, he'd feel the cold hardness of the cuffs being secured around his wrists. And she'd continue on her way without so much as a backward glance.

No, the straightforward approach would not work without using specifics. And if he did that, he automatically went back on his word to Dr. Whitney.

This choice did not sit well with him. He had been raised to believe that giving your word was the only significant thing a person had to give. It was so strongly ingrained in him that he had an intense feeling of guilt knowing what he might have to do to succeed. But the more he thought about it, the more he believed that Catherine was in real danger. Keeping his word to Dr. Whitney might no longer be an option. He hoped the doctor would eventually come to accept his decision, especially if his choice involved saving someone's life.

After all, wasn't that the exact same thing Dr. Whitney had done for him?

He went over every possible explanation of how he knew what he knew. Each time he did he failed and failed miserably, the complexity of what he had committed himself to do was getting the better of him. With each try he found himself adding bits and pieces about the operation to provide credibility to his story, and that was exactly what he had hoped to avoid.

Michael practiced out loud, as if he were actually addressing Catherine in person. He was totally convinced that the images he had been experiencing showed her life was in jeopardy, but he was not so sure he would ever be able to convince her. He doubted he would be convinced if approached by a stranger with a story such as his.

After many hours of practicing a skillful presentation, he decided it would be almost impossible to engage Catherine long enough to fully explain the seriousness of the situation. Still, Michael always returned to one conclusion: she was in danger, and he was the only one who could do something about it. She had to be warned.

He paced back and forth in his small living room. Drained, he eventually settled himself down on the comfortable couch, placed his hands behind his head, leaned back, and closed his eyes.

Clearing his mind, he relaxed a little more. Unexpectedly, a whole new approach came to him. He was amazed by the simplicity of it. Maybe he had been making everything harder than it needed to be. Over and over he played the new scenario in his mind. *This has to work*. For the first time in a long time, he was confident that he might actually be able to pull it off.

He now had a definite how, all he needed was a definite where, but with someone as high profile as she was, that would be the easy part. Sitting in the fading light of his living room, he realized he was smiling.

Chapter 32

Garrett slowly opened his eyes, his head pounding with pain as he surveyed the room where he had spent the last several days. *God, what a pigsty.* He reached over to the nightstand, hoping to find a cigarette. Instead, his hand met with some unidentified substance.

"Shit!" he exclaimed, attempting to wipe it off on the sheets surrounding him.

Totally disgusted, he sat up in a haze. *I need a cigarette.* He turned again toward the nightstand, a plate of congealed uneaten food sat precariously on the edge; just looking at it turned his stomach.

He carefully peered over the side of the bed, hoping the ache in his head would not increase, and spotted a cigarette pack lying on the floor next to his pants. Gingerly, he swung his legs over the edge of the bed and rubbed his face with his hands. The urge for a cigarette definitely took precedence over the pain in his head. He bent down gradually and grabbed it, realizing by its weight that it was empty. Angrily, he crushed it in one swift crunch.

I've got to get out of this place. He reached for his jeans and dressed hastily, not really caring that his appearance made it quite obvious he had not showered for days. Garrett shoved his hand into a pocket. It was empty. He checked the other three. They, too, were empty. No cigarettes, no money.

"That bitch," he growled, his voice barely audible. His rage was instantaneous and uncontrollable. He rushed down the stairs, burst through the beaded doorway, and into the darkened bar.

Chrissy was unaware that Garrett had entered. She was too busy working the room and had found a potential customer ready to pay for her talents.

Garrett waited for his eyes to adjust to the darkness. Spotting her at the end of the bar, he headed in her direction.

"You bitch. You stole my money!"

Chrissy looked up at the sound of the angry voice. Garrett was on her, blind with rage. Before she had time to scream, he had his hands wrapped tightly around her throat. She fought with all her strength, but it wasn't enough.

The bartender came around the bar and jumped in attempting to free Chrissy from his murderous grip. Garrett felt his hands being torn away from Chrissy's neck, but before she was totally free he threw her backward with such force she fell, the back of her head squarely hitting the edge of the table. Warm blood flowed from the gash, instantly making bright red streaks in her overly bleached hair. Someone pulled her upright and applied pressure to her open wound while Garrett continued to wrestle with the bartender. Even though Garrett was the smaller of the two men, he held his own by the sheer intensity of his anger.

"Call the cops!" someone yelled.

"No! No cops! Do you want to be busted?" Chrissy hissed. "Eddie can take care of it."

But Garrett was like a madman, no longer feeling dazed from the night before. His instincts were as sharp as an animal in the wild, toying with its prey. He was getting the best of Eddie, making him look like a fool in front of his regulars. Eddie shoved Garrett across the room and quickly slid his hand into his boot, pulling out all the protection he and the girls would ever need.

Garrett bore the entire force of Eddie's shove. It took all the effort he could muster to stay on his feet. He lunged straight in the direction of his foe. Someone behind him call out, "Knife!" The click of the blade snapping into place instantly changed his game plan.

His part of the fight was over. He was not crazy enough to believe he could overtake someone with a weapon. Instead of continuing forward, he spun his body around and bounded out the door. He doubted anyone would follow him. He was not sure where he was going, but it didn't matter. All he really wanted was a damn cigarette.

****

"Hello, Mrs. Paxton. This is Detective Costanza."

"Yes, Detective?"

"He's all right."

"Thank God."

"Mrs. Paxton, he's heading down Broadway. I'll keep an eye on him and let you know where he goes."

"Thank you so much for the news, Detective," Catherine said, relieved that Garrett was alive and had yet to do anything too foolish.

"Anytime, ma'am," he said politely. "I'll be in touch."

Chapter 33

"Honey, I don't think this benefit luncheon will last more than a few of hours." Catherine stood in Tamara's doorway, trying to secure the clasp on her gold charm bracelet.

"Here, let me do that for you," Tamara volunteered, noticing her mother's difficulty.

"Thank you." She smiled. "I always have such a hard time with this one, but it's one of my favorites."

"Mom, are you sure you don't want me to take your place?" Tamara asked, concerned.

"No thank you, sweetheart."

"You know, you don't have to do this. People will understand."

"I know they would, but it's time for me to get out and do the things I enjoy doing."

Catherine had founded the Theresa Cavan Foundation in honor of her friend who had died of AIDS. It became quite obvious to Catherine that Theresa's friends, family, and society as a whole appeared to have no tolerance for the disease and especially for those who contacted it through an extramarital affair.

Catherine was appalled at the treatment her friend had received by others. Right or wrong, Theresa was her friend. Catherine was one of only a few who stayed by Theresa's bedside and she was one of a mere handful who attended the funeral of the once vivacious and important woman.

She waged a long hard battle to get the foundation off the ground, and under her direction the foundation flourished. Its success ultimately led to building of the Theresa Cavan Hospice. Catherine continued to remain involved with the foundation on one level or another, and nothing would keep her from attending its major fundraiser.

"You know, I'm actually looking forward to seeing the new spring fashions that are going to be shown at the luncheon today. Though, I was hoping to have a chance to stop at the caterer's and swing by Madame Russo's to pick up our dresses on the way"—Catherine glanced at her watch—"but I don't think I'll have time to do both."

"I'll be glad to pick up our dresses."

"We could have them delivered, but I know how busy they are this time of year. I really don't mind picking them up myself."

"Really, Mom, it's no problem. I'll pick them up tomorrow on my way in to the office."

"Are you sure? I know you are busy too."

"Would you not worry about that and finish getting ready, or you really won't have any time to stop at the caterers. And I wouldn't even dare attempt to do that for you." Tamara smiled.

"Okay, okay." Catherine mimicked her daughter's sarcastic smile. She knew her well-known obsession to detail intimidated many, and sometimes even her daughter.

"Go!" Tamara urged, gently pushing her toward the door.

She heard Tamara laughing as she disappeared down the hall and into her own room. Things were finally beginning to feel normal.

****

Michael believed he knew exactly where Catherine would be. After spending some early morning hours at the library reading everything he could find about her, he was positive she'd make an appearance at the Theresa Cavan Foundation charity luncheon. She hadn't missed one yet. Gleaning as much information as he could, Michael found he had gained both admiration and hopefully a little bit of insight for this woman he had yet to meet.

He believed going to the luncheon would be his best chance to speak with her. It couldn't be done before the luncheon, there would be reporters all over the place, something he definitely hoped to avoid.

Instead, he decided he would attempt to make contact with her as she came out, before she was picked up or got into her car. He really didn't know how she would be traveling, which could actually complicate things. In order to have even the slightest chance of success, he needed to get there early and figure out how and where he was going to approach her.

Once back at the apartment he showered and dressed with care. He had to look as if he fit right in. The very last thing he wanted to do was call attention to himself before he even had an opportunity to approach her.

****

Everything was going well with all the preparations for the Scottford Ball and Catherine was pleased. She knew her mother and father would be proud of the way she had continued their philanthropic tradition. Thinking of them and the upcoming ball filled her with mixed emotions.

Life had not been easy the last couple of years. People she loved had come and gone, but she was thankful for what she still had. She had her health, her business, her daughter, and somewhere out there, her son.

Her thoughts clouded. *Where was he?* She hoped he was all right. No matter what he had done, she wished he would surface again soon. Not knowing was the hardest of all. Still feeling a sense of loss, she stepped into the limousine waiting for her just outside the caterers.

"To the luncheon, Maxwell."

"Yes, ma'am," he said and promptly shut the door behind her.

Chapter 34

He arrived early enough to enter unnoticed with the usual assortment of florists, caterers, and sound men, all busy completing their specific tasks. Michael scanned the enormous room in awe. Spectacular flower arrangements were everywhere. That fact wasn't so amazing, but the overwhelming abundance of them in the middle of winter certainly was. It made him wonder if a single fresh flower was left anywhere else in the city!

He remembered reading about Theresa, who had loved to surround herself with flowers, all kinds of flowers. And that is exactly what they had accomplished. Every seat in the room appeared to be positioned as if you were sitting in a garden in the middle of spring.

So caught up in the grandeur, Michael was not aware that he was calling attention to himself by appearing to have no purpose for being there.

He caught a glimpse of a security guard heading in his direction. Realizing he had just made his presence very precarious, he methodically started to move toward the front doors. The guard followed.

I can't believe I did this. Several beads of sweat dripped down his back and soaked into his shirt as he continued on. Hesitantly, Michael glanced back. The security guard had picked up his pace. By the sound of quickening footsteps the distance between them was closing. Any minute now, he expected to feel the forceful grip of the man coming up behind him.

His mind raced, trying to come up with a plausible explanation for being there, but he couldn't think of anything. His reasoning skills were frozen in sheer panic. He could not imagine what he thought he was doing and the stupidity of the situation he now found himself in.

Finally making it to the front entrance, a sense of relief swept over him. But that feeling was a bit premature, as a strong hand clamped down on his shoulder. He stopped instantly. It was over. Everything he had so meticulously planned was destroyed by giving in to his powerful sense of curiosity.

He turned to face the security guard, but before he could, he was gently moved aside.

"Excuse me, sir," the voice said with obvious authority. "I need to get through. There seems to be a problem out front."

"Of course." Michael said, quickly stepped out of the way, hoping the guard wouldn't notice how nervous he was. He could not believe his luck, as the guard rushed past him. Not wanting to risk discovery any further, he headed out the front doors right behind the security guard.

Reporters were everywhere. A fight had erupted between two cameramen who argued over being first at a prime location in which to film the arrival of the local celebrities.

The ensuing commotion made it easy for him to slip through the people and equipment. He positioned himself toward the back of the crowd in an attempt to catch a glimpse of Catherine without being too obvious.

He settled himself just in time to see the first limousine pull up. He watched as the mayor's wife stepped out smiling and waving to the crowd. Immediately, the press converged on her. Car after car made its way to the curb by the entrance. Renewed interest rose each time the doors of the next limousine opened and its occupants emerged.

Michael observed even the smallest detail in silent anticipation. A jet black limousine took its place in line about three cars down, and he instinctively knew this was her car. His body felt as though it was gearing up for something. He recognized the warning signs, but this time he was not about to let his anxiety take over. With all his concentration, he closed his eyes and focused. *She needs to be warned and I am the only one who can do it.* It was that simple.

A cheer went up around him. When he opened his eyes, he was looking straight in the direction of Catherine Paxton. She turned slowly, greeting those around her. She was exactly the same as the images he visualized in his mind, right down to those intense blue eyes. He knew at that moment he had made the right decision, regardless of the outcome.

As quickly as she had appeared, she disappeared into the building. Michael's chance was fast approaching. He decided there was no reason to stand out in the cold with the other onlookers. He had seen what he had come for, now it was a matter of timing.

He hurried down to the parking lot and got inside his car. It was too cold to sit there, so he turned on the engine and flipped on the heater. Soon the interior was comfortably warm. When the temperature reached the point of being almost too warm, he turned it off. He would have to do this many more times before his waiting was over.

Chapter 35

The telephone rang in Catherine's study and by the sound of it, Tamara could tell it was her private line. She knew that if she didn't answer it, no one else would. She got up from behind her desk, which now sat in the center of the massive room she used to consider foreboding.

Looking around, she liked what she saw. Gone was the big brown leather chair. In its place sat a sleek Scandinavian piece, which suited her small frame. The heavy drapes that had hung above the elegant windows were replaced with crisp white shutters that remained open much of the time to let the sun's rays light the room naturally.

The room also sprouted greenery from every available space, something not seen previously. The only piece she had kept was the family portrait, which still hung on the wall behind the desk.

No matter what her father had turned out to be, he was still her father. She came to terms with the fact that a part of her would always love him. And that part of her made her decide to keep the portrait where it had always been.

The persistent ringing of the telephone jarred Tamara from her thoughts. She quickly crossed the hallway and entered her mother's study. She grabbed the receiver, hoping she wasn't too late.

"Hello?"

"Oh, hello. I wasn't sure if anyone was at home." The surprise in his voice told Tamara he didn't expect anyone to answer. "Didn't want to bother her on her cell phone, only wanted to leave her a message…Oh, and this is Detective Costanza," realizing he hadn't given his name. "Is Mrs. Paxton in?"

"No, I'm afraid she's out right now. May I take the message, Detective?"

There was a hesitation on the other end.

"It's all right for you to tell me, really it is." Tamara tried to alleviate any fears he might have breaching some sort of confidentiality. She continued. "I know my mother hired you to track down and keep an eye on my brother."

"I wanted to let her know that Garrett has disappeared again."

Her heart sank, knowing her mother would be truly disappointed by this news. "Are you sure?"

"Yes, ma'am."

The displeasure in his voice was obvious. "Detective, if it makes you feel any better, I know my brother will surface again. He always does, especially when he needs something."

"I believe that, too, ma'am. But it's been a little harder to keep track of him than I'd expected."

"Well, don't let it bother you too much. My mother was quite aware that her request was not going to be easy. Anyway, I'll give her the message."

"Thank you."

"Oh, and Detective, happy New Year's," she said, hoping to lighten his mood.

He laughed. "You, too, Miss Paxton."

Chapter 36

Michael awoke to the sound of car engines starting. Geez, he was cold. His fingers and nose were numb. Still groggy, he looked out the frosted window. The cars were already pulling out of the parking lot. He turned and looked in the direction of the main entrance. The line of limousines had already formed.

"God, I hope I haven't missed her." He bolted from the car, through the parking lot and back up to the main entrance.

The steps and surrounding area were clear. Most of the press had gone, though some were milling about creating opening pieces or background shots. Several small groups of women stood together talking while waiting for their cars.

Michael looked around. He didn't see Catherine in any of these groups, but she had to be there. *Please, let her be here*, he prayed. And just as if someone had heard his prayer, Catherine emerged through the entrance and descended the stairs. He swallowed hard. It was now or never.

"Excuse me, Mrs. Paxton," he called out, heading in her direction.

"Yes, may I help you?" She turned toward him.

They looked directly at each other. Michael froze. He was stunned by the intensity of her blue eyes.

"May I help you?" she repeated.

"Yes...uhh, I'm Steven... Steven Malloy with the *Peninsula Preview*." He extended his hand forward to shake hers.

With a questioning look, she extended her hand to meet his. Reading her hesitancy, Michael quickly went on. "We are a very new...and very small paper. We are also in the process of developing new areas of interest for our readers. Hopefully, it will expand our current circulation." He laughed as he made the last comment. She, too, seemed amused at his candidness.

Encouraged, he continued. "If you could spare a few minutes of your time, I would greatly appreciate it."

"I would be glad to, Mr. Malloy."

"Thank you," he replied. *But now what?* Stalling for time to collect his thoughts, he fished out a pen and a notepad from inside his coat pocket and poised it as if he were about to write.

She looked at him oddly.

"Oh, I prefer old school," he said as he held up the pen and notepad.

"Yes, well I've done a bit of research on this charity luncheon...and by the looks of it, it was quite a success."

"Yes, it appears so." She smiled at his well-placed compliment.

"Do you believe this endeavor has been the best to date?"

"It certainly was a very good one. These charitable events have seemed to increase the public's awareness and compassion for the disease and those who are affected by it. I hope this education and acceptance will continue to move in this positive direction for many years to come."

"Though we have made significant strides, do you believe there will ever be a cure?"

"I hope so."

"Me too," he quietly agreed, rubbing the side of his nose. Michael knew he couldn't hide behind this charade forever, he needed to move on. He pushed forward. *Here goes.*

"I know this question is a bit off the subject...and stop me if it's too..."

Catherine eyed him cautiously. "Go ahead, Mr. Malloy. Ask your questions."

"I understand your husband was recently killed in an automobile accident," he began, nervously trying to lay some ground work.

"That's correct."

"It was reported earlier that a there may have been an issue with the mishandling of funds, which could possibly affect the stability of your family's corporation. Is there any truth to this?"

It was obvious that Catherine was well rehearsed for this line of questioning, she took a deep breath and responded in a tone that conveyed an extreme lack of concern. "Yes, there had been some speculation; however, Scottford Textiles has been, and is currently, prosperous for its investors. The corporation remains under the watchful eye of the same board of directors who continue to keep Scottford stock solid. There is absolutely no reason to be concerned about the corporation's stability, even in today's economy."

He kept his head bent, jotting down notes on the open note pad, trying to look authentic.

"Uhm, getting back to the death of your

husband..." Michael was losing ground. He knew what he wanted to ask but was afraid to do so. Taking a deep breath and without looking up, he continued. "It is rumored that, at the time of his death, his license confirmed his consent for organ donation." He paused, then blurted out what he needed answered. "Is that true?"

Once it was asked, he couldn't take it back, nor could he continue on in this vein, because if he did all the promises he had made to Dr. Whitney and to himself would be broken.

There was dead silence. *Please, just give me this one answer I need.*

"Yes, he did, but what does that have to do with Scottford Textiles?"

"Well, I oh, uhm...I'm doing a piece on donor authorizations on licenses and how they are the most underutilized method of saving lives. If...uhm...if it was true, I could use it and...uhm... I know the readers would be interested in this sort of thing." Michael's attempt to try and pull everything back together was failing miserably. Slowly, a frown of apprehension formed on her face.

"Well, Mr. Malloy, I need to get going now." She started moving down the steps toward the waiting limousine. He followed her until she had reached the last few steps and was only a few feet away from her car. If he didn't do something quickly she would be in the car and the opportunity would be lost forever.

"Mrs. Paxton, someone intends to do you serious harm," he said in a clear, but not loud voice.

Catherine stopped, as if she was not sure what to do next. Looking around, she again began to move forward.

Without thinking he reached out and gently gripped her arm in an awkward attempt to prevent her from leaving. He felt her tense.

"I am not that person."

Catherine turned, facing him directly. They again looked straight into each other's eyes, this time with heightened intensity. It was obvious she was not afraid of him.

"I wanted to warn you. I can't explain how I know, I just do."

Catherine said nothing for a moment.

"You need to be careful, very careful, Mr. Malloy." Her eyes narrowed.

"Mrs. Paxton, is everything okay?" Maxwell called out to her. He had been standing at the side of the limousine observing Catherine and the young man speaking with her.

"Yes, Maxwell." She looked questioningly at Michael. "Everything is fine, right?"

Michael nodded and let go of her arm. Catherine immediately turned and headed for the waiting limousine, hastily disappearing into the back.

Michael moved to the sidewalk outside Catherine's window. He stood motionless, watching the long car pull away from the curb.

Chapter 37

Catherine came through the front doors, pulling off her gloves as she moved. Noting the light on in her daughter's study, she smiled. *That child of mine is so much like her father in so many ways, it's almost scary. I am so thankful it was his most admirable traits she inherited.*

As she headed for the stairway, she decided to stop in and see what Tamara was working on. "Hello, dear. You seem to be very busy."

Tamara looked up from her cluttered desk and smiled at her mother. "Hi, I didn't hear you come in. You look exhausted. How'd it go?"

Catherine sat down on the peach-colored love seat that faced Tamara's desk. Looking around the room, she smiled. *This is exactly what I would have done with this room.*

"It was quite a day. You should have come with me."

"And miss all this?" Tamara chuckled as she mockingly swept her hand across the top of her desk. She leaned forward toward her mother. "So tell me everything."

"It was beautiful, absolutely beautiful. Theresa would have loved it."

"I know she would have, Mom."

Catherine went through the day's events. By all

accounts, everything had gone extremely well. Then her thoughts turned to her meeting with Steven Malloy. She absentmindedly slid the shoes from her feet. She was tempted to tell Tamara about the strange encounter but decided against it. Her daughter didn't need another worry in her life right now. She was still trying to convince herself there was nothing to worry about.

Tamara watched her mother. "Mom, Detective Costanza called."

"What? Oh, I'm sorry, sweetheart, I was still thinking what today's success will mean to the foundation. What were you saying?"

"Detective Costanza called. Garrett has disappeared again."

Catherine shook her head in disappointment. "I hope he's all right."

"I'm sure we'll hear something soon. Detective Costanza seems to be very conscientious about his work. I could tell he was not very happy about losing Garrett."

Catherine stood. As she did, she looked down, noticing that her shoes were off. She looked up at her daughter, who was watching her with great interest. Realizing she had just signaled her daughter that she had other things on her mind. Catherine scooped up her shoes and headed from the room, mumbling something about her new shoes hurting her feet more than she thought they would.

****

It's time to do a little homework, he thought as he confidently walked into the spacious lobby. Without hesitating, he headed straight to the registration desk, taking note of the strategically placed security cameras and the overhead signs announcing the location of the ballrooms. The fake mustache irritated his skin and the padded suit weighed heavily on his slim frame, but the discomfort was only temporary. With check-in complete, no one took any notice of the heavy-set man with the mustache making his way into the crowded elevator and up to his room.

Chapter 38

Michael felt like a total failure. It had seemed like such a good idea to approach Catherine as a reporter, not an uncommon situation, gain her confidence, and then tell her he had overheard an unidentified person make a threat to her safety. He had planned to tell her as little as possible, while advising her to take some extra precautions to ensure her safety. He had rehearsed it so many times that it should have been simple, but in his nervousness and impatience, he had gotten off track. After that little scene, there was no way she believed any part of what he had said to her.

Disheartened, he slumped down on the old familiar couch. *Now what? I waited so long for this opportunity and I blew it. Totally blew it! It's over; it has to be.*

He sat there for a while, realizing how tired he had become. His body hurt, probably from sleeping in an odd position as he had waited in his car. He decided to take a long, hot shower and call it a night.

Half an hour later, he gratefully climbed into bed. In some ways, he was relieved that he was finished with it all. It was time to move on with his own life. After such a stressful day, he assumed it would be easy to fall asleep, but it wasn't. Again and again he replayed the afternoon's little fiasco in his mind.

Catherine was a beautiful woman, but what really made a lasting impression on him were her flashing blue eyes. The clarity and wisdom he had seen while speaking to her was evident. It was obvious that she had fought her personal demons and had definitely come out the victor.

After meeting her, Michael convinced himself that Catherine was a strong, capable woman who could take care of herself. Finally drifting off to sleep it didn't take long before a picture of her formed in his mind. He heard voices. He heard the soft music. He had heard this music before.

Michael was experiencing another image. He didn't want to, he wanted to be done, but it was obvious he was not. So this time he prepared himself to ride it out, no matter where it took him. Catherine was standing right in front of him in a shimmering glow. He had been this far before and waited for the images to move forward.

He again found himself standing alone in a maze of color. The voices were getting louder, laced with anticipation. Michael recalled the first time he had made it this far. He needed to look up. As he did, the music hit a chord of announcement and the sky filled with the same illuminating colors that surrounded him. The colors began to drop toward the ground.

He heard screams of delight as the image continued, exactly as it had before. The colors grew closer and closer. When they were within his reach, ear-shattering popping began startling him with their intensity. He could not make any sense of what was going on around him.

Confused, he turned to head in another direction. There was another sound, one that was distinctly different from the constant popping around him. He was not sure what this new sound meant, but it seemed to intensify his need to find Catherine. She was there somewhere and he would not allow himself to be released from this image until he found her.

Michael could not see anything. Desperately, he called out her name, moving forward through the sound and color. He spotted her lying on the floor. Her body gave off an iridescent glow. He approached slowly, not sure he really wanted to see what was before him. Then the noise suddenly ceased. It was eerily quiet. As much as he had hated the irritating popping sounds, he found the silence much more unnerving.

He moved closer to her body and knelt beside her, calling her name softly. She did not respond. He gently took a hold of her shoulders and shook her, but her eyes did not open. He felt for her pulse but found none.

With a start, Michael opened his eyes to total darkness. He had finally seen the image through to its end. He knew Catherine's intended fate and realized his part in all of this was not yet finished. This last image solidified his resolve to make another attempt to warn her. No matter how hard he struggled with his decision, he now knew there was no way he could keep his word and attempt to save her life.

Chapter 39

Tamara quickly descended the stairs and into the solarium, knowing her mother would be there enjoying her morning coffee.

"Morning, Mom," she said cheerfully.

"Good morning," her mother replied, lifting her head from the newspaper. "Sit down and have some breakfast with me."

"Can't. I have so many things to take care of before I get to the office."

Her mother scowled at her and her eating habits. "Tamara…"

"Okay, okay. I'll have some of your toast," snatching the first thing within her reach. "Goodbye." She kissed her mother on the cheek and headed out of the room. "And thank you," she added, waving the half-eaten piece of toast above her as she headed straight to the front door.

Catherine shook her head and laughed at her daughter's juvenile gesture.

****

Michael did not sleep well. He awoke feeling like he had not slept at all. He got up and made his way to the bathroom. Catching a glimpse of himself in the mirror surprised even him.

"My God, I do look like I could be a psychotic killer," he said staring at his reflection. His eyes were red-rimmed and puffy. A day's worth of stubble had appeared on his usually clean-shaven face. His hair was almost standing on end from the night's constant tossing and turning.

Michael headed to the kitchen to make himself a cup of coffee. He was at a loss of what to do next, but he was positive of what the outcome would be if he did nothing at all. This was the first time an image had reached completion, and he did not like the way this one had ended. Time was running out, he was definitely sure of that.

The idea of breaking his word to Dr. Whitney was still so objectionable, but he didn't see any other way. He couldn't stand by and allow this terrible thing to happen to the beautiful Mrs. Paxton with the startling blue eyes. He renewed his pledge to follow through with finding a way in which to warn her.

Michael was now convinced, more than ever, that he needed to persuade Dr. Whitney to confirm his story. Without the doctor's help he was certain his failure would be repeated. Reluctantly, he got up from his chair and called the familiar number.

"Dr. Whitney's office, may I help you?"

"Yes, I would like to speak with the doctor."

"I'm sorry, the doctor is unavailable right now. May I take a message?"

"Could you please tell him that Michael Peterson called and needs to speak with him? And please tell him it's urgent." He rattled off his number and thanked the receptionist.

He had barely hung up when the phone rang.

"Hello?"

"Hello, Michael," said the familiar voice. "Is

everything all right?" Michael could hear the genuine concern in the doctor's voice.

"Everything's fine. At least for me."

"So what can I do for you, Michael?"

"I just need you to hear me out."

"Go ahead."

After Michael finished explaining what had happened over the last few days, Dr. Whitney spoke.

"I understand your dilemma, and I respect you for trying so hard to uphold your part of our agreement, but after all the years I have invested in this project, and then finally having the opportunity to see how successful it would be on a human patient..." his voice trailed off. "I simply can't help you."

Michael had surmised this would be the doctor's response, but he had to give it one more try. Clearly disappointed, he asked, "Doctor, if by some remote chance I get someone to actually believe me enough to check out my story with you, could you please reconsider your decision and provide them with some sort of confirmation?"

There was a pause on the other end.

Michael could tell his passion to do the right thing was beginning to wear on the doctor. It had become something he didn't have to do but was compelled to do. Just like the doctor, he believed he was trying save a life.

"I'll consider it." Michael could hear the doctor's resolve slipping.

"Thank you, Dr. Whitney. Thank you so much. Goodbye."

With that hurdle somewhat cleared, Michael decided he would go see Catherine directly and somehow make her listen to him. He would do it today.

****

Stepping from the elevator, Tamara tried hard not to drop any of the precious packages she was carrying. Hearing her struggles, Grace rushed to assist her, taking several packages from Tamara's overburdened arms.

"Thank you." She sighed with relief.

"You're welcome." The older woman smiled and followed Tamara into her private office.

"Put them anywhere," she said, carefully hanging the beaded gowns on the old-fashioned coat rack standing in the corner. "You've got to see these, Grace." Excited, she uncovered the beautiful gowns.

Grace completed stacking the last of the packages and turned obligingly to admire the gowns that Tamara had been describing to her for the past few months.

"Oh, Miss Paxton, I don't think I have ever seen anything quite as lovely as these." She lightly touched the delicate beads on one of the dresses.

"Aren't they perfect?"

"They truly are. You and your mother will make stunning Geminis."

"And," Tamara said gleefully, "I had another great idea to make the illusion absolutely flawless." She whispered into the woman's ear as if they were being watched.

"What a marvelous idea!"

"Now don't you go telling my mother," Tamara tried to sound stern.

"Cross my heart," Grace replied solemnly, mimicking the promise with her finger. Both women laughed simultaneously at the comical gesture. "Is there anything else I can do?"

"No, but thank you so much for helping me get all this stuff in here. I have to pick up a couple more things, but I'll do that at lunch."

"Okay, let me know," she reiterated and returned to her desk in the outer office.

Tamara again turned her admiration toward the beautiful gowns, her excitement growing. She had not anticipated how much she was actually looking forward to the event.

She stood there silently watching the blueish-green crystals catch the sunlight and throw sparkling patterns on the far wall of the office. She loved the effect so much, she hated to cover them up. But if she didn't, she wouldn't get anything done. With a sigh of disappointment, she replaced the cover on the dresses and sat down at her desk to start on the day's work.

Chapter 40

Garrett didn't know how, but he had made his way back to his apartment. It wasn't much, but since his father had cut his allowance to a couple of thousand a month, it was all he could afford. He climbed the stairs and went directly to his door, but could not get in.

"Shit," he said out loud, knowing his pockets were empty. "I don't have a key."

Garrett headed down to get a spare key. He crossed the courtyard and pounded on the manager's door.

"Donnie, lemme in, it's Garrett," he yelled as he continued pounding. "Come on, open up!"

Donnie opened the door a crack and saw Garrett standing there. Then he opened the door all the way.

"Man, where you been?"

"Out. Need a new key." He glared at being questioned.

"No problem." Donnie got one of the spares and handed it over to him.

"Thanks," Garrett mumbled and turned to go back up the stairs "Wait, I got some mail for you. Your box was full, so the mailman dropped these off here."

Garrett took the stack of mail and mumbled something inaudible. Reaching his apartment, he entered and immediately searched for cigarettes. There had to be some somewhere. Frantically he searched through the kitchen drawers, getting madder with each unsuccessful try. He jerked open the last drawer and was rewarded with not one, but three unopened packs. He had hit the jackpot! After tearing open a pack and smoking two cigarettes back-to-back, he sat down and calmly lit a third.

Garrett started to go through the stack of mail. Most of it was junk, which he tossed aside without even opening. Toward the bottom of the pile, he came across a perfectly square envelope. His name was engraved on the front.

He tore it open, destroying the envelope as he pulled out an invitation with a moon and star on the front. He had forgotten all about the annual charity ball and laughed as he read the inscription. The timing could not have been better. *How kind of them to jog my memory*. He began contemplating how he could use the situation to his advantage.

His mood lightened, recognizing what opportunities this little piece of paper offered him. He got up from the table and stuffed the invitation and the two unopened cigarette packs into his pockets.

Garrett left his apartment, he laughed at his sudden twist of good fortune.

"Thanks for the invite, Ma! I'm so glad I'm still on the A-list."

****

A frightened Donnie dug out the man's card, who'd come by the apartment a day earlier, saying he was a private detective looking for Garrett Paxton. Donnie had been reluctant to say the last time he had seen Garrett, being the kind of guy who didn't want to be involved in anybody's business. The detective had assured him that no one would ever know he had provided him with any information. Donnie was still not convinced, until there was some mention of the possibility of a reward. That was all he needed to hear. Who didn't need some extra cash these days?

Minutes after Garrett's appearance, Donnie called Detective Costanza. It didn't take long before the detective returned to Donnie's front door and Donnie eagerly pointed out Garrett's apartment. The detective went straight to his door and knocked.

Nothing happened. Donnie watched the detective through the small gap in his kitchen curtains. After knocking several more times he turned back toward his apartment. Though he was not the brightest person, he knew what the detective was going to ask him to do. He also knew it was against the law to allow someone to enter a tenant's apartment without a warrant.

****

Detective Costanza smiled. It wasn't as hard as he had expected. All he had to do was mention the possibility of a reward again and the key was handed over, no questions asked.

He slowly opened the door to Garrett's apartment, not really knowing what he would find on the other side. He checked room by room but found nothing unusual. It was messy, but it had all the markings of someone with money. Massive leather furniture and a huge entertainment center boasting an obscenely large flat screen, with a multi component sound system that was connected to each room.

The kitchen looked more disheveled than all the others. All the drawers were open and their contents were thrown haphazardly onto the countertops. Both opened and unopened mail lay scattered across the table. The smell of a recently lit cigarette hung in the air. *Damn,* he had just missed his quarry.

Ready to leave the apartment, he looked around one more time, and noticed a torn envelope lying under the table. He picked it up and looked inside. It was empty. He turned it over. It was some sort of invitation, and Garrett's name was engraved on the front. Detective Costanza immediately recognized the return address.

He returned the key to Donnie and thanked him for all his help, letting him know that there might or might not be a reward as Garrett was nowhere to be found. Donnie's frown told him what he thought about that, but Detective Costanza didn't care; he needed to contact Mrs. Paxton. His gut feeling told him that the envelope he was holding was a not a very good sign.

Chapter 41

Making his way through the busy streets of the city, Michael felt his apprehension beginning to build by the quickening of his heartbeats. The sun shone brightly for this time of year as once again he found himself looking up at the imposing Scottford Textile Corporation building.

This is it, he told himself as he entered the lobby. He noted that the marble floors still shone and that the security booth was still manned. *The security booth*, he groaned inwardly. *How could I have forgotten about that? How am I going to get past security?* He wished just once something would work out in his favor.

He checked his watch. It was a quarter to twelve. He looked back at the booth and noticed a second man in a security guard's uniform approaching the glass enclosure; they were switching for lunch. He calculated the distance between himself and the elevator. *If I time it just right, with a little luck on my side, I might be able to make it into the elevator without detection.*

He moved toward his goal. Blending in with others who were moving in the same direction, he put his head down and kept going. His heart was pounding, and continued to do so even as he stepped safely inside. Finally, the doors glided shut, protecting him from discovery.

He made it, but it wasn't over yet. There were four

other people alongside him. Michael stood very still, not wanting to make eye contact with any of them. The man and woman on his right were deep in conversation. The two on his left stood quietly. Michael patiently waited as the elevator climbed. One person got off on the sixth floor, a second on the fifteenth, and the couple who were oblivious to anything around them got off on the twenty-seventh floor.

The doors shut at last. He was alone. He reviewed at the panel board, but he had no idea which floor he wanted. After staring at the multitude of buttons for what seemed like a long time, he pushed the one marked thirty-two. He decided that is where he would have his office if he ran a company as prestigious as this one.

The elevator moved upward and arrived at its destination more quickly than he had anticipated. When the doors opened, he found himself stepping into an impressively decorated outer office and knew he was in the right place.

"May I help you, sir?"

"Yes, I would like to see Mrs. Paxton."

"Do you have an appointment?"

"I… I…well no, I don't." He stammered and rubbed the side of his nose.

"Well, I suggest that you call and make an appointment."

"Please, I only need a few moments of her time."

"I'm really sorry, sir, but you will need to make an appointment. Now, if you would please leave."

"No, I really need to see her now." He persisted.

"Please, sir, you need to leave or I will have to call security."

"Then you'll have to call them." Michael stood his ground.

"I guess we will," said a voice from the other side of the room. Both heads immediately turned in that direction.

With purse in hand, sunglasses on, Tamara had opened the door to the scene taking place in front of her.

"Can I help you?"

Michael's attention remained on the small blonde framed in the doorway, but he quickly glanced back at the woman behind the desk. She had not made a move to pick up the phone.

Feeling a little more secure in his part of the stand-off, Michael turned back.

"My name is Michael Peterson, but Mrs. Paxton, you may remember me as Steven Malloy. You know, from yesterday? I spoke with you at the luncheon?" He tried to get some sign of recognition out of her. "I really need to speak to you in private"—he glanced back again in Grace's direction—"regarding what I said to you yesterday."

There was no response.

Michael was confused; surely she remembered him? There was no way she couldn't.

"Oh yes, Mr. Malloy, I mean Peterson…yesterday at the luncheon," she answered, nodding as she continued, "Won't you come into my office?"

Tamara led him into her office and closed the door. "Please, have a seat," she said, offering him the chair in front of her desk.

"Thank you. I see you were on your way out so I won't take up too much of your time."

"It's no problem."

With her short answers and Michael's nervousness he didn't pick up on any of the slightest subtleties of difference, even though he sat directly facing her, with only the distance of a desk between them. He cleared his throat. "As I was saying, Mrs. Paxton, I sincerely believe you are in danger," he stated matter-of-factly, wanting to convey the serious nature of his visit.

"And tell me again why you believe this?" she asked. Her voice held obvious skepticism. He saw an eyebrow rise above the rim of her sunglasses and knew he had better move on quickly with his explanation.

"I know because…because…"

"It's all right, Mr. Peterson. Please, go on."

Michael carefully explained as much as he could without disclosing any details about the operation. Knowing the information he gave her was not going to be enough to satisfy her once she had enough time to think it through, he still had to try it this way first.

"So, let me see if I understand everything. Someone has threatened my life, but you don't know who this person is?"

He nodded. "That's correct."

"If you don't know who the person is then how can I verify my life has been threatened?" He could tell by the tightness of her voice she was fighting to stay calm, as she requested confirmation of his flimsy explanation.

Michael moved uneasily in his chair, knowing he would have to tell her at least a small portion of the truth for her to believe even a part of what he was about to say. He chose his words carefully. "Do you remember when I asked you about the donor card on your husband's driver's license?" He asked, absentmindedly running his finger down the left side of his nose.

The question seemed to throw her off, but after a pause she answered. "Yes…"

"Well, that signed card allowed an experimental operation to take place."

"And?"

Letting out a deep breath, Michael continued. "And I received a grafting of your late husband's brain cells." He stopped, letting his last statement sink in, then realizing the sheer absurdity of what he had just said, he decided to move on quickly before the opportunity was lost.

"I know this is hard to understand, but it's true and for some reason yet to be explained, I have also gotten bits and pieces of his memory. I see images, and…"

"Wait a minute; wait a minute." Tamara shook her head and put a hand up. "Stop right there. How…"

Before she could finish her question two security guards burst through the office doors. They were at least two-and-a-half times Michael's size, and could have been offensive linebackers in a previous life. Without uttering a word, Michael was slammed up against Tamara's desk, his arms painfully twisted behind his back. There was no way he would be walking out on his own volition.

"I'll go, I'll go." Michael squeezed out a response from his prone position.

Tamara stood there looking at the helpless man held against the top of her desk.

"Would you like us to call the police, Miss Paxton?" one of the guards asked.

Michael struggled to pull his head up from the

desk. "Miss? *Miss* Paxton?"

Tamara slid her sunglasses down to the tip of her nose. "Yes, Miss Paxton," she confirmed.

With that Michael was unceremoniously jerked up to a standing position and found himself looking directly into her beautiful green eyes. Only then did he believe that he had not been speaking to Catherine Paxton and the person in front of him was in fact, Catherine's daughter. *The resemblance was uncanny.*

He and Tamara stared unflinchingly at each other. He would not back down; not this time. For a fleeting moment Michael felt as though they had somehow connected, and on some level she might have actually believed him. As bizarre as his story sounded, he saw confusion cross her face, but there was something else, maybe confusion mixed with a little spark of belief that what he had said could indeed be plausible. That was all he wanted.

"Excuse me, Miss Paxton, do you want us to call the police?"

"No. See that Mr. Peterson is escorted out of the building."

"All right, buddy, let's go." The head guard grunted angrily, roughly yanking him toward the door.

Before they had a chance to turn him away from her he said, "Please contact Dr. Whitney. He'll explain everything. He'll confirm what I've told you. Anyway, I hope he will…"

"Come on, come on," the guard barked. He turned Michael around and shoved him toward the door.

As he was forcibly escorted past Grace, Michael had one more idea that might help him prove his case. "Ask her about a box, a black metal box, the one in the bottom desk drawer." He motioned his head in the direction of Tamara's office, though he was not sure Grace actually heard him, as she was desperately trying to get around the three of them and into the office.

****

Once inside Tamara's office, Grace found a distraught Tamara sitting in her chair.

"Miss Paxton, are you all right?"

Looking up at the older woman's face, Tamara could see that she was concerned. "I'm fine," she said quietly, trying to allay her fears. "But I think I'll go home for the day."

"I think that's a good idea. Would you like me to call you a driver?"

"No, that's not necessary. But if it's not too much trouble, could you please have someone deliver my packages to the house?"

"It's no trouble at all, Miss Paxton. They'll be delivered before the end of the day."

"Thank you." Tamara began to gather some of her personal belongings going through the motions without much awareness of what she was actually doing.

"Are you sure you're all right?"

"I'll be fine." Tamara patted the older woman's arm and headed out the door.

****

Driving around for the next couple of hours, not paying attention to where she was headed, Tamara was at a loss. She was glad she had not immediately intervened in the exchange between Grace and Mr. Peterson. That brief confrontation provided her with enough information to conclude he'd intended to meet with her mother. She knew it wasn't right to deceive him, but the more she listened, the more intrigued she had become. She needed to know just what this Michael Peterson had to say.

Was her mother really in danger? Her mind jumped to the unusual explanation Michael had offered for knowing what he did. *If he wasn't telling the truth, then how did he know about her father's donor card? Could there possibly be an operation like the one he had described?*

She doubted it, but he had given her a name, the name of the doctor who had performed the operation. *God, what was his name?* She tried to remember. *Dr. Whitely? No, that wasn't it. Doctor...umm...Doctor Whitney. She was sure that was it.* Finding the doctor would certainly add credibility to his bizarre story.

Her thoughts went back to the man in her office. Why would a man who apparently wanted nothing from her—or should she say, her mother—take such a risk, and such a personal one at that? Not just once, but twice. Twice he had tried to approach her mother. That was actually quite gutsy when she thought about it, because her mother was one of the most influential women not only in San Francisco, but in the world. That said one of two very distinct things about this Michael Peterson: either he was truly convinced someone was going to do her harm, or he was stark raving mad. No wonder her mother did not tell her about their meeting. It was too strange to believe.

Tamara pictured his earnest brown eyes. She could tell he believed his story, and he desperately needed her to believe it too. The only way she could put her doubts to rest was to find out how he knew what he did. Then she'd know if her mother was actually in danger, and it might also prove that Michael really wasn't a kook. But somehow she already knew Michael wasn't a kook.

It was getting late. She needed to get home and wanted to talk with her mother. She glanced at her watch, surprised it was already after five.

Well, she wouldn't be able to contact this Dr. Whitney today. She regretted that she hadn't tried earlier, but she planned on it first thing in the morning.

Chapter 42

Michael tried to stretch out his arms, but they were still sore from being pinned behind his back. He couldn't believe that Mrs. Paxton turned out to be Miss Paxton, and he never had a clue. She had shown no fear in dealing with something that seemed beyond rational explanation, nor did she appear to be fearful of him. Just like her mother, she displayed a strong sense of who she was.

He pictured her intense green eyes. They were every bit as incredible as her mother's crystal clear blue ones. He remembered feeling an instant connection, or at least he thought he had. If she'd only think through what he had said she would surely come to the conclusion there just might be some legitimacy to his claims. For her mother's sake she had to!

What else am I feeling? If he was honest, in that brief meeting he felt much more for her than he wanted to admit. He was uncomfortable with the feelings she stirred in him. It seemed almost incestuous. Besides, it would only complicate things, and things were already complicated enough.

Well, he was glad it was over. He had done what he had set out to do. They were warned and now it was up to them to ensure Catherine's safety.

Satisfied he had done all that he could, he decided to go out and celebrate. He put on his jacket and left his apartment, heading toward Sausalito to enjoy dinner at a new little Italian restaurant he had read about. Not having been there before, he took the easiest way he could navigate. His little car climbed its way up to the Golden Gate Bridge. Soon he became keenly aware that this choice might not have been a good one. His body tensed, his heart started to race.

Traffic was moving fast. Michael switched lanes, trying not to get caught in the slower traffic. He didn't see that the cars in the next lane had begun to slow down also. He was going too fast.

"Oh my God, I don't believe this. Not me. Not now!" The words came out of his mouth, but the voice did not sound like his. He glanced at both the side and rearview mirrors, taking in the cars around him.

Frantically, he tried to slow down, but he couldn't. The car seemed to have taken on a life of its own. Michael suddenly realized what was about to happen, but he was determined not to let history repeat itself. Gripping the steering wheel with both hands and using all his strength, he forced the car to veer onto the pedestrian walkway. He held the wheel in that position, controlling the car's movement until the passenger side of the car made direct contact with the concrete guardrail. Upon impact, the air bags deployed and the car came to a screeching halt.

Badly shaken, but not hurt, Michael sat behind the wheel. He was thankful to be alive and grateful that no one had chosen that moment to take a stroll across the bridge. He got out of the car and noticed an emergency phone a few feet away. But before he even got there, the sirens in the distance already informed him they were heading in his direction.

****

When Tamara arrived home, anxious to speak with her mother, she realized that this, too, would have to wait until morning. Finding her mother's room empty, she went to her own room and found a note on the bed.

Tamara,

Didn't want to bother you at work, but wanted to let you know I'm meeting with Detective Costanza this evening, as something new has come up involving your brother. The detective appears quite concerned about our safety, though I am not. Please don't worry. I'm not sure what time I will get in, so there is no need for you to wait up for me.

Love you,

Mom

P.S. The gowns and assorted packages were delivered this afternoon. You were right when you said they were perfect. They are absolutely lovely! See you soon.

****

After spending over an hour answering questions and taking those humiliating sobriety tests, he was free to go. The accident was attributed to mechanical failure. He watched as his little car was towed off for repairs.

With all that had transpired, Michael decided to put off his celebration until another time. Within minutes he was able to flag down a taxi. Riding back into town seemed to take so much longer than it had to get out to the bridge. When he finally arrived home, he paid the driver and quickly entered his apartment, wondering what else could possibly happen.

Chapter 43

"But I am concerned about your safety," he repeated.

"Detective, I appreciate your concern, but we're talking about my *son*." She emphasized the last word.

"I understand that, ma'am, but I don't think this is a good sign." He pulled the crumpled envelope from his coat pocket and placed it on the table.

Catherine picked it up. It pained her to see there was still so much anger and hostility deep inside Garrett. She hoped that with the death of his father and the passing of time, Garrett would have lost some of his passion for hatred. But seeing the elegant envelope mangled told her this was not the case. And she didn't believe it was likely to get any better in the near future either.

She looked across the table at Detective Costanza. For as much as she did not want to admit it, he was right; it was possible that Garrett could become dangerous. "All right, Detective, you can station some men at the ball, but no more than four."

"Okay."

"Oh, and one more thing." She smiled before she went on. "Your men will need to be in costumes."

"Are you serious?"

"Quite."

Though her blue eyes sparkled with humor, she

was not kidding. "I don't want my guests to be alarmed by the sight of plain clothes men posted around the room. We have worked too hard to see that this event is successful. It would be tragic to have it ruined by any kind of a threat, be it real or imagined."

"I understand, Mrs. Paxton."

She decided to throw in another request that would surely make him groan out loud.

"And Detective, they need to be dressed in costumes reflecting the Zodiac, something to do with the various constellations"—she smiled sweetly—"or the planets."

He looked at her, unable to comment. He started to shake. His whole body was in motion. Maybe she had pushed a little too far? Watching him move, she suddenly realized he was not angry at her, he was laughing. She started to laugh with him.

Between bouts of laughter he added, "My men are going to love this one."

****

Even though her mother had said not to, Tamara decided to wait up for her. She ate a light dinner, grabbed a good book and a blanket, and lit the fireplace in the living room. She knew her mother would stop in on her way up to bed.

Tamara stretched out on the living room couch, pulling the soft blanket around her. The room warmed; she felt cozy and safe.

The grandfather clock chimed in the hallway. It was nine o'clock. *Where is she?* Tamara wasn't worried, she just wanted her to get home so they could talk. She had so many questions she needed answered.

Tamara was so comfortable, she never even

attempted to open her book. The clock again chimed on the hour, but this time she did not hear the count.

****

Quietly, Catherine entered the house. A light on in the living room surprised her; she didn't think anyone would be up this late. She crept into the room and found her daughter sleeping peacefully on the couch. A blanket lay beside her on the floor. Embers glowed in the fireplace and the room had a slight chill.

Catherine picked up the blanket and covered her daughter, kissing her gently on the forehead. "Good night, sweetheart," she whispered and left her daughter in undisturbed slumber.

Chapter 44

Michael awakened early. He had his usual cup of coffee and then decided to take a brisk walk to clear his head.

As he walked, he replayed what had happened the night before on the bridge. He shuddered, realizing how close he had come to reliving the donor's death scene. No matter how much he wanted to deny it, a part of Elliot Paxton had been there with him. Michael felt Elliot's panic rise inside him. He had heard Elliot's voice coming out of him. He was aware he had lost total control of everything around him.

At that very moment Michael knew he was going to die, yet something inside rebelled and refused to let it happen. When he placed both hands on the wheel and pulled some kind of inner strength took over, forcing the car to its ultimate resting place.

He had been lucky, and he knew it. Did this recent demonstration of his own power and control possibly indicate the diminishing of the images? He really didn't know, but it made him feel good thinking that he might have gained a little bit of control over his life again. Completing his fourth time around the block, he decided to call the garage to see just how much his newfound strength was going to cost him.

****

"Aren't you going to work today, sleepyhead?"

Catherine teased as she placed a silver tea set on the coffee table in front of her daughter and sat down on the couch beside her.

Tamara rolled over and peered at her mother, attempting to shoot a look of disdain in her direction.

Catherine laughed. "I've got plans for you today," she announced, "but you will have to tear yourself away from this cozy little bed you've made for yourself here."

"What time is it?"

"It's almost ten."

"Ten!" Tamara sat straight up.

"Don't worry, I've called the office and told them you wouldn't be in today."

"Thanks." She leaned back against the arm of the couch, propping herself up.

"It was rather strange when I spoke with Grace to let her know you wouldn't be in today. She seemed overly concerned about your well-being."

"What makes you think that?" Tamara asked, wondering just how much Grace might have told her mother about yesterday's little incident.

"She really didn't say anything specific. She just asked a few questions about your health. It was not like her, that's all."

"Oh, she's just getting on in years, and health seems to be a major topic of conversation."

"You're probably right. It just seemed odd at the time."

"Let's have some coffee," Tamara said, trying to create a distraction. She poured two cups and handed one to her mother.

"Thank you."

"You're welcome." Tamara hesitated, not knowing how to approach the subject that was on her mind.

"Mom, I need to talk to you about something, something that happened yesterday. I met a man named Michael Peterson." Tamara could see that mother had no idea who Michael Peterson was. "You met him the day before as Steven Malloy."

By her mother's immediate reaction, Tamara could tell her mother knew exactly who that was. Catherine looked inquisitively at her daughter. "How did you meet him?"

"He came to the office, and in the beginning he mistook me for you. Well, actually I let him believe he was talking to you, because he mentioned speaking with you at the luncheon. I wanted to know what he had said."

"He got into the office, your office?" Tamara could tell by her mother's tone she was not pleased with that fact.

"Yes, but…it was all right. Nothing happened."

"And what exactly did he say to you?"

"He said he spoke to me, I mean…, you…at the luncheon."

"Yes, that is where I met him."

"He said that he had warned you that someone was going to harm you." Tamara hesitated, watching her mother's face for a fearful response, but none was forthcoming. "Aren't you concerned by what he said?"

"No, I'm not. Living in the public eye is not an easy way to live. Through the years, there have been numerous threats made toward our family. The majority of these have proven to be harmless."

Tamara heard a certain sadness in her mother's

voice, accepting she was no longer a young girl who needed her protection.

"You and your brother were always protected and were never exposed to these incidents. Your father and I worked very hard to shield you from the harsh realities of being in the spotlight. Now that you're running the company, I'm sorry to say you will probably see many things that you never knew existed."

Her mother was right; she had indeed lived a sheltered life. Was this man a threat? He certainly didn't seem like one at the time. He came across as so earnest and sincere. There seemed to be a yearning for her to believe what he was telling her. But his story about the operation was a bit farfetched, even in this day of medical advancement.

Tamara decided not to tell her mother the rest of what Michael had said. It was too unbelievable, and her mother didn't need to hear it. But why had he continued to approach them?

"So, do you think this man wanted something from us?"

"Yes, I do. Eventually, he would have gotten around to asking for money or possibly a favor. I think in each of his attempts to speak to us, the opportunity to request something was probably cut short by the circumstances."

Tamara saw the logic in what her mother was saying and nodded in agreement.

"Anyway, sweetheart, if it makes you feel better, I will have this Michael Peterson checked out." She patted her daughter's arm affectionately, then rose. "I'll call Detective Costanza right now," she said and started to leave the living room. With a smile, she added, "But you, lazybones, need to get moving."

Tamara sat thinking about what her mother had said. She was probably right. There was no real reason for her to be alarmed, but even so, something still did not feel right and she decided she was going to do a little bit of checking on her own.

Chapter 45

"Detective Costanza, this is Catherine...Catherine Paxton." She blushed when she realized how presumptuous she had been, expecting him to recognize her by first name only.

"Hello, Mrs. Paxton. What can I do for you?"

"I have a favor to ask of you."

"Shoot."

"Could you please do a quick check on a Michael Peterson?"

"Sure. Is there a problem?"

"No, I'm just curious. Oh, and Detective Costanza..."

"Yes?"

"I had a wonderful time last night," she confessed somewhat shyly.

"I did too."

****

"Hello, my name is Tamara Paxton and I would like to speak with Dr. Whitney."

"I'm Dr. Whitney's nurse. Can I help you?"

"No, I need to speak to the doctor directly," she said nervously, still not knowing exactly how to pose her questions.

"Hold on, please. I'll see if he's available."

What am I doing? This is crazy. There was absolutely nothing credible about the things Michael

Peterson had said. But there was a genuine sincerity about him that made her want to follow through with his request. What could she ask this doctor without sounding like a fool?

"This is Dr. Whitney." A warm voice came from the other end.

"Hello, Doctor. My name is Tamara Paxton and I'm calling to get some information on the feasibility of a specific type of operation."

"Go ahead, Miss Paxton."

"Doctor, is it at all possible that the cells from one person's brain be grafted into the brain of another person?" She held her breath, not sure which answer she wanted.

"No, I don't believe the kind of operation you are describing is possible."

She let out her breath. "That's what I thought. Can I ask you one more question?"

"Sure, go ahead."

"Do you happen to know anyone named Michael Peterson?"

"No, I'm pretty sure I do not."

She sighed. "Okay. Thank you very much for your time, Doctor. Sorry to have bothered you."

"No bother at all, Miss Paxton."

****

When her mother told her what she had planned, Tamara was all for a day of pampering. Together they agreed it was just what they needed to be relaxed and ready for the ball the following evening.

It felt good lying perfectly still with the cool, drying mud spread uniformly over their faces, their hands encased in mitts filled with moisturizer.

It was hard for Tamara to hide her disappointment after her call to Dr. Whitney. No matter how outlandish the operation had sounded, she had hoped there might be some truth to what Michael Peterson had said.

She was usually a pretty good judge of character, but boy, she was way off on this one. Her mother was right. He was simply another opportunist looking for an easy mark. And she could kick herself for almost being one.

Tamara glanced over at her mother who appeared to be lost in her own thoughts.

On the drive over Catherine had said that Detective Costanza had done a check on Michael Peterson and he had come up clean. Not even so much as a parking ticket.

This fact seemed to disturb her mother more than if several pages of offenses had come up. She explained that the ones trying to pull a fast one usually had some sort of history with law enforcement, but oddly this one did not.

Her mother had gone on to explain that more often than not the facts never panned out as anything more than an idle threat or some feeble attempt at extortion. She was convinced this too was nothing to worry about.

Even with all her mother's explanations and the call she had placed to the doctor, Tamara was still not totally convinced there was nothing to this.

****

He viewed himself in the full-length mirror. *This is exactly what I was looking for.* The costume fit him like a second skin. Dressed like this, no one would be able to tell who he was. The sense of anonymity made him feel powerful.

After trying on several costumes, he settled on Draco, the dragon constellation. Having dabbled in the occult, he knew that Draco also represented the Tarot trump card for Death. He liked the connection.

The leotard was hand painted in numerous shades of green, from a deep forest to a silver gray green. Small scales had been painstakingly outlined in gold. The uninterrupted pattern ran down the back and continued around to his sides.

On the front, a frosty green filled in where the scales left off. Dark green lines ran across his chest and stomach area to represent deep crevices on the underside of a dragon's body.

The part of the costume he really liked was the mask. When placed on his head, the mask came down to just below his cheek bones, then jutted outward, forming a dragon's snout with long pointed teeth. The eyes were cut in deep angles giving off the illusion that the dragon was angry.

Attached to the back of the elaborate mask was an abundance of sheer strips of delicate silk in the same hues as on the leotard. The mask completely concealed his identity, ideal for what he had planned. All he needed now was an opportunity to get close to Catherine. One chance was all he needed.

Chapter 46

By the end of the day, Tamara was totally relaxed and ready to face the ultimate fundraising event of the season. She could tell her mother was too. On the way home, they stopped for a light dinner. The evening was pleasant, though they were both uncharacteristically quiet, keeping their conversation limited to the upcoming ball. It was dark when they arrived home. They said their good nights and headed to their rooms.

****

Once in her room Tamara began organizing the packages that had been dropped off the day before. She unwrapped each box, making sure everything was ready for the next day. When she got to the last package, she carefully opened the lid and lifted out two burgundy jewelry boxes. Inside each box were identical opal and diamond earrings. She held them up to the light. They glistened with the same brilliance as their gowns. Tamara tried on one earring. *It's perfect, just perfect.* She admired her choice in the mirror. During their last trip to the Orient they learned that opals symbolized loyalty and hope, something she knew was much needed in her mother's life right now. Taking the earring off and placing it back in the box she was glad she had decided to get them. Her mother would love them.

Tamara looked around the room. There should be

one more package, but she didn't see it anywhere. It had to be there. Where could she have left it? After thoroughly searching her room, she went downstairs and checked around. The package was nowhere in the house.

Back in her bedroom, she sat down on her bed. She retraced her steps, trying to remember the last time she had seen the package. All she knew was that she had picked it up at the same time she had picked up all the others.

It must have been left at the office. That was the only place left to look, but she didn't want to drive into the city tonight to see if it was there. She would have to go in the morning. Her mother would not be pleased, but she had to have that package.

****

He sat in his darkened car, careful not to let the glow of his cigarette be seen. He noticed the nondescript car parked in the alley with a shadowy figure inside. His apartment was being watched.

That bitch. He didn't know if he wanted to con her or kill her. Nope, killing her would be too easy, and that wasn't the outcome he wanted. But if by some remote possibility she'd revised her trust and excluded him, giving everything to his sister… The anger that thought instantly ignited definitely left murder as an option.

There would be absolutely no way he would be able to con his sister. Tamara was the only person with enough insight to see him for exactly what he was, and that was not good. The thought of his sister with all that money and power infuriated him.

It would be much more entertaining to try and win his way back into his mother's good graces, watching his sister squirm as he did it. For as well as she knew him, Garrett understood her also. Knowing how fiercely loyal she was to their mother, he was confident she would never go against him if Catherine accepted him back into the family.

He was satisfied with his decision, knowing he had all that he needed right in his car. He started up the engine, and without turning on his headlights, backed down the street, turned, and sped away.

Chapter 47

"Good morning, Miss Paxton. I didn't expect to see you today." Grace couldn't hide her surprise.

"Good morning. I hadn't planned on coming in, but somehow I misplaced a package and wanted to see if it was here at the office. I know I could have called, but I really wanted to check for myself."

The women entered the large office and looked around but didn't see the small package anywhere.

"Darn," Tamara mumbled. "Where could I have put it?" In desperation she got down on her hands and knees and looked under her desk and across the floor.

"There it is!"

"Where?"

"Under the couch."

Grace walked over, bent down, reached under the couch, and grabbed the small package.

She placed the package in Tamara's hands. "Now, you better get home and start getting ready for the ball."

"Thank you. Oh, and about the other day…"

"You don't have to discuss any of that with me. I'm just glad you're okay. I was a little worried when you didn't come in yesterday."

Tamara sat down. "No, I do feel I need to let you know what happened. It was all so weird. I really don't know where to begin." She recounted the conversation she'd had with Michael Peterson.

"You know, you took quite a risk by asking him into your office." Her tone was disapproving. "And then shutting the door!"

"I'm sorry. I didn't mean to scare you, and I know this is going to sound really strange, but I don't feel as if I took any kind of risk at all. I think Mr. Peterson is the one who took a risk, a big one." She added, "I wish I had more information to go on…"

Grace twisted her hands together. "I don't know if I should tell you this, but before Mr. Peterson was removed from the office, he said something about a box, a black metal box that was here in the desk."

"There *was* a box," Tamara said excitedly. "I found it when I was cleaning out my father's office."

"Where is it?"

"It's at home, in the basement with the rest of the things I took out of here!" Tamara could barely contain herself.

"I've got to go. I've got to try and find it." Glancing at her watch, Tamara realized she didn't have much time to search.

Making sure the small package was secure she quickly headed for the elevator. Stepping through the opening doors Tamara heard Grace call out, "Good luck, and have a wonderful time tonight."

"I will, and thank you, Grace; thank you for everything!"

****

Michael could not believe he had actually made it through an entire night without an image reappearing. He felt rested for the first time in a long time. Maybe it was really over and he was finally free of his self-imposed mission.

When he called the garage, the mechanic said the car was going to take quite a bit of work to get all of the damage repaired, but it could be driven if the metal was pulled away from the tires to prevent it from rubbing. Many of the needed parts would have to be ordered and they would take at least a week to come in.

He decided he would drive the car in the meantime until it could be totally repaired. After making his way to the garage and picking it up, he wasn't sure what to do with the rest of his day.

It was New Year's Eve, and he had nothing to do and no one to share it with. Not that it really mattered. His life was so mixed up right now, he would hate to subject someone else to it.

He would do what all self-respecting single people do; he would go to the delicatessen and buy some outrageously priced snacks to stock his refrigerator. Then he would sit in front of the television and watch the ball drop in New York City, signaling the end of the old year and the beginning of the new one. Michael hoped the next year would be better than this one had turned out. And yet, he was truly thankful he had lived to see the end of this year.

****

Even with the small overhead light on, the basement was dark. Tamara frantically searched for the metal box.

"I know it's here somewhere." She had just finished going through the contents of the fourth storage box. She looked hopelessly at the other five in front of her. Her heart sank, realizing there was no way she'd have enough time to search through them all.

She opened the next one within her reach. All it

contained were books. She shoved it aside, already knowing this was not the box she had put it in. Tamara stood up and rubbed her aching arms. "Okay, Tamara just keep going," she said as she pulled the next one toward her and knelt beside it.

"Tamara. Tamara, where are you?" Her mother was calling.

"Down here!"

"Down where?"

"I'm in the basement."

Catherine opened the door and flooded the room with light. "What are you doing?"

"Uhhhh, I'm looking for...for an old ledger I thought might be useful, I'm sure I put it in one of these boxes when I cleaned out Dad's office." Tamara hated lying to her mother, but it was just a little white lie that could be fixed later if her hunch was correct.

"I'm sure what you're looking for must be important, sweetheart, but you need to come up and start getting ready for the ball."

"Okay, Mom, I'm on my way." She knew her mother was right. A strong punch of disappointment coincided with the realization her search would have to be postponed.

As Catherine turned to leave, Tamara looked at her watch. She had time to go through one more box. She opened the lid and lifted out miscellaneous items. Toward the bottom, her fingers touched something cold. Her heart raced. She pulled out an empty tape dispenser and several well wrapped coffee cups that were hindering her attempt to get at the object trapped below.

At last, she was able to slip her hands down and

around the smooth, cold sides of the object. Without even looking, she knew it was the metal box she had taken out of her father's desk.

She sat back on her heels, holding the black box straight out in front of her with both hands. She bit the side of her lip as she stared at her find. *Well, here goes.* She held her breath and tried moving the latch. It was stuck. She tried again, but it still didn't budge. It was obviously locked. She couldn't believe it. After all this, she couldn't open it.

"Damn," she said aloud and shook it, listening to the contents inside. It sounded like papers. Frustrated, she tried several more times to slide the catch, but no matter how many attempts were made the catch would not move. Nothing was going to get her what she wanted.

Disappointed, she set the box aside, got up and dusted off her knees. It would have to wait until tomorrow. She started to leave the box there, then thinking better of it she turned back, grabbed it, and headed up the stairs.

Chapter 48

From a short distance away, he patiently watched and waited until he could enter the hotel unnoticed. As in all his commissions—he liked to think of them that way—he was not only very meticulous in his selections, he put in extremely long hours of fastidious background work to make sure each job could be executed without incident. He had turned down very few in his career, because rarely was there a job that he couldn't do. Each job presented specific risks, but it always boiled down to was timing and no matter what, his timing was impeccable.

This one was proving to be unique, not technically, but by the mere fact that dogs had actually been brought in. *A bomb? Too messy.*

The dogs were led over the grounds every half hour, sniffing. This went on for several hours; each time they picked up a new scent, several men teamed up and headed off right behind the barking dogs, but they always came back seemingly empty-handed. Once they had completed their last round, the dogs were loaded into a truck and taken away, he took the opportunity to enter the hotel.

Once again heavily disguised, he proceeded calmly across the lobby, now bearing the weight of his weapon concealed in the folds of his clothing. He was keenly aware that security reinforcements had been brought in and that worried him. Did they know about the threat? There was no way they could; his communication with Elliot was untraceable.

After making his way to his room he remained there until dusk. He used his time to methodically review his plan, mentally walking through each phase of what he was about to do minute by minute. The plan was perfect, he saw no flaws, but a slight feeling of foreboding remained. For the first time in his career he decided to ignore it.

As the time drew near he exited his room, making sure the security cameras could not catch a clear picture of his face. He traveled down the hallway refraining from anything that would call attention to himself.

Planning for this job had been interesting. He learned that the older hotels were not built with the same standards as the newer ones and they were not always uniform, which worked to his advantage. One or two doors always remained just slightly out of the full scope of the cameras. To catch every little nook and cranny down long twisted hallways was nearly impossible. For this particular job it had only been a matter of figuring out just which floor offered him that one true blind spot.

He turned a corner and slipped into a utility closet, already knowing that this door in this particular hallway happened to be just outside the camera's view. Once inside he deftly unscrewed the heavy metal screen that covered the vent. With the screen grasped in one hand, he climbed up, squeezed in, and secured the screen back on to the vent behind him. He stripped off his padded suit and with weapon in hand, crawled forward, easing himself through the complex venting system. He knew exactly which direction he needed to go.

****

He watched silently from his cramped space as the finishing touches were made in the ballroom. A huge ice sculpture was brought in and carefully placed in the center of the main table. Large silver platters of food were strategically set on each side. Next to them rows of silver chafing dishes were being placed in their stands, while golden candles were simultaneously lit around the spacious ballroom.

After completing the final inspection, the event coordinator gave the go-ahead. The double doors were swung open. He could hear the oohs and ahhs of the costumed figures as they entered the beautifully decorated ballroom.

Time was drawing closer. Even though his client was dead, he still had a job to do. And while nobody would be the wiser if he didn't follow through, that wasn't his style. His choice of profession might be questionable, but his reputation was not.

Chapter 49

They stood next to each other, the light catching the iridescent beads on their gowns. The crystals that hung from their headpieces seemed to illuminate their delicate features.

The illusion was astonishing.

Tamara could see her mother was pleased with the effect Madame Russo had created. She was glad she had talked her into doing this, dispelling any doubts her mother may have had dressing as twins.

"Mom, you look gorgeous," Tamara said admiringly.

"And you do too," Catherine replied.

"Cute, Mom." Tamara laughed.

"Well, sweetheart, we need to get going." Catherine picked up the matching beaded bag from her dresser.

"Wait just a minute. I have a couple of things to do before we go."

"All right, but please don't be long. Maxwell has been waiting with the car for the last twenty minutes."

"I'll hurry," Tamara promised and headed for her own room.

"I'll wait for you downstairs," she called out to her disappearing daughter.

Once inside her room, Tamara picked up three small boxes. She slipped one box into her own beaded bag and clutched the other two tightly inside each hand.

Leaving her room, her gaze fell on the black metal box sitting on the chair next to her bed. She was positive it held the answers to many questions, but those answers would just have to wait.

****

Tamara walked gracefully down the sweeping staircase. She caught a glimpse of her mother's gaze and the pride reflected in her eyes as she descended the stairs into the entryway.

Jeffreys stood alongside Catherine. "You look lovely, Miss Paxton." He gently placed Tamara's shimmering cape upon her shoulders.

"Thank you, Jeffreys." Turning toward her mother, she handed her one of the small burgundy boxes.

"What's this?"

"Oh, just something I picked up," she said lightly, knowing that her mother would not miss the true meaning of her gift. "Open it."

Catherine opened the box slowly, enclosed were an exquisite pair of opal and diamond earrings, tears intensified the brightness of her blue eyes.

The center stone was the exact same bluish-green color of their costumes. Speechless, unable to express the love she felt for this kindhearted gesture, a tear slipped from her eye.

"Mom, don't cry, you'll ruin your make-up," Tamara said, seeing her mother's reaction. "Besides, they're not one of a kind," she joked. "See?" She quickly popped open her box and showed her mother the identical pair.

Catherine laughed at her daughter's revelation and leaned over and kissed her on the cheek. "Thank you, they're beautiful."

Quickly, they took turns securing the precious gems in their ears, using the delicate antique mirror that hung in the entryway.

"You both look stunning," Jeffreys said candidly.

"Thank you." The words came out at the same time, and the three of them laughed.

"It's time to go," Catherine announced.

"Now I'm ready," said a smiling Tamara.

"Have a wonderful time." Jeffreys jokingly made a sweeping bow and ceremoniously opened the front door for them.

"We will." Again they responded in unison and headed to the waiting limousine.

As the door closed behind them, the phone in Tamara's study rang. On the third ring, the answering machine automatically clicked on.

"Hello Miss Paxton, this is Doctor Whitney. I do know Michael Peterson and he is telling you the truth."

Chapter 50

This was going to be easier than he had anticipated. He had been able to walk right in and blend with the other guests without so much as a sideward glance from the security stationed at the front door. All it took was an elaborate costume and an invitation in hand. And that little detail had been unexpectedly provided by the friendly postal service.

Everything was so elegant. Small white linen-covered tables were placed intimately around the room. Each table was adorned with golden accents. The mirrored walls held the glittering reflection of the ornate candelabras that had been lit and set into place.

One side of the room held a culinary extravaganza of gourmet foods, set out buffet style. The centerpiece included a six-foot-high crescent moon sculpted from ice. It was surrounded by an array of golden lights shaped into stars. Even the smallest of details had been seen to.

Toward the back of the spacious ballroom, the archway doors opened to allow guests an opportunity to stroll among the gardens. In the Grand Ballroom a four-tiered chandelier sparkling with gold and crystal hung in the center of the room. The rest of the ceiling was completely concealed with a cloak of midnight blue fabric. Woven into the dark material were the many constellations of the night sky. The effect was quite dazzling.

He slowly walked across the room, taking in everything, finally selecting what he felt was the best vantage point. Now all he had to do was wait for the right moment to make his move.

****

Something did not feel right to Detective Costanza, and without getting Mrs. Paxton's permission, he placed several more men outside to secure the grounds. Even with the extra precautions, he was still uneasy. Something was going to happen. He didn't know what or when, but he was not about to take any chances on this one. He had to be content with overseeing the operation from outside the main entrance, since there was no way he would put on a costume himself. He walked the lobby and the beautifully manicured grounds of the hotel, hoping that for once his gut feeling was wrong.

****

The limousine pulled up in front of the hotel. Tamara looked through the tinted windows at the throngs of media waiting outside the hotel's main entrance.

"Mom, I need to stop at the ladies' room before we make our entrance."

"Really Tamara. Now?" Impatience crept into Catherine's voice.

"Sorry." Tamara shrugged. "It will only take a minute. Please, one quick stop. I promise."

"Okay, sweetheart. One...quick...stop."

They exited the limousine, and Tamara was blinded by flashing cameras. She stopped and smiled in all directions. Charming the press was something both knew how to do, and for this event, they did so effortlessly.

When they finally got inside, Tamara slipped into the ladies' room and was back at her mother's side within minutes. "Okay, I'm ready."

"That was quick."

Tamara walked with her mother through the main archway and paused at the top of the steps that led into the grand ballroom. The master of ceremonies announced their arrival. All movement in the room ceased and everyone turned in their direction. Drawing in a deep breath, Tamara took her mother's hand as they descended the steps.

All eyes were on them. Catherine squeezed Tamara's hand and gave a small, satisfied smile, no doubt pleased with the reaction of their guests. They had accomplished exactly what they'd hoped to.

A group of elegantly costumed well-wishers swarmed them, and Tamara was soon separated from her mother, but not before she caught her mother's eye. Catherine smiled, giving her a nod of approval. The illusion was complete.

Chapter 51

Michael settled in for the evening's festivities. He had dined on a gourmet sampling of his favorite deli's fare and was ready to spend the rest of his fun-filled evening in front of his new television watching the traditional dropping of the ball in Times Square.

Seeing the freezing masses in attendance in New York, he was glad he lived on the West Coast.

He decided to catch the eleven o'clock news before channel surfing. With nothing particularly interesting on the news, he got up and cleared away his dishes. From the kitchen sink, he could hear the newscaster.

"Good evening, this is Jean Beardsley reporting live from outside the Lexington Hotel. We were able to catch a few of our local celebrities as they made their way inside the Grand Ballroom for this year's Scottford Charity Ball. The costumes have been extremely creative this year, but I would have to say the most spectacular costumes were worn by the Paxtons. Both Catherine and Tamara..."

Even the sound of the running sink water could not drown out the names Michael knew so well. He rushed back into the living room and watched the screen intently.

"Here they are as they arrived earlier this evening," the voice said as the recap video played. "Aren't their costumes fantastic?" You could hear the sense of awe in the newscaster's voice as she continued on with her description.

As mother and daughter turned toward the cameras and smiled, it was not the crystal blue eyes or the sparkling green ones that caught his attention; it was the colors of their costumes that seemed to explode across the screen. Michael instantly recognized the colors as the same ones he had seen in the images. He had not stopped anything. Catherine was going to die tonight.

Michael grabbed his coat. He didn't know how he was going to get into an invitation-only party, and a costumed one at that, but hopefully he would figure that out on his way there.

****

With only thirty minutes until the New Year, Tamara and Catherine stood in front of the microphone.

"Ladies and gentlemen, if we could have your attention, please." Catherine paused, waiting for everyone to quiet down. "First, I would like to say on behalf of myself and my family, thank you so much for coming tonight. You all look superbly celestial."

A spontaneous round of cheers and applause went up at her acknowledgment.

"Thank you. Thank you so much." Catherine put up her hand to again quiet the crowd. "At this time, baskets are being passed around with golden crescent moons in them, like this." She held up the little moon. "Please take one."

"And be careful," Tamara added. "The points are a little sharp."

"Now I know that you have been waiting to find out how you were going to donate this year. Well, my daughter and I are going to demonstrate. Tamara?"

Accompanied by a drum roll, a single teal-colored balloon dropped from the sky into Tamara's open hands. As she held it the crowd waited in silenced anticipation. Catherine took the golden moon and pricked the balloon. Breaking the quiet in the room with a loud pop, golden star-shaped confetti and a small slip of paper drifted down to the ballroom floor.

Tamara gracefully caught the slip of paper in mid air. Everyone cheered. She held it up, smiling.

"Written on each slip of paper will be the amount you must donate, though you can donate more if you choose to do so. At midnight, the sky will open up and balloons will drop from above. Catch one, pop it, and find out what size donation you are being asked to give."

The crowd was getting louder.

"Oh, and one more thing," Catherine said, playing on the anticipation. "The person who donates the most over and above their donation slip will have a newly discovered star named in their honor or of someone they may choose to honor." Again, applause erupted.

"Hey, Catherine," a voice cut through the clapping, "what does your slip say?"

"Tamara," She motioned her daughter forward.

Tamara stepped up to the microphone and opened the slip of paper. She smiled coyly at the crowd.

"It says," she paused for effect, "the sky's the limit!"

The room rippled with laughter. As it died down, Catherine again moved in front of the microphone.

"Again, I want to thank you all for coming. We are truly appreciative and deeply touched for all your support. Have a wonderful evening."

As she and Tamara left the stage and entered the crowd, they passed an ominously costumed figure who had moved in closer for a better view.

Chapter 52

As Michael got closer, he had yet to come up with how he was going to get into the ballroom. He pulled his car into the public garage, parked, then quickly walked the last few blocks to the Lexington Hotel.

The hotel was quite impressive and definitely out of his league. Climbing the main stairway and walking through the lobby, Michael immediately took note of where the ornately costumed figures were entering and exiting. He headed in their direction, but once he got closer he stopped, seeing how well guarded the entrance to the ballroom was, not only by uniformed guards, but also by several plain clothes men trying to blend in. Was the extra security placed there because of his warning? He hoped so.

Knowing there was no way he would get in through the open doors in front of him, he turned and headed back through the lobby, down the stairs, and out on to the sidewalk. He continued walking, rounded the corner and headed down the block, trying to determine if there were any unguarded points of entry. Nothing looked too promising. He looked at his watch. Ten minutes until midnight. He had only one chance to get to Catherine, and if he didn't make it, he was sure she would be killed.

Coming to the end of the building, he turned and walked back up the street, heading toward the side of the hotel where deliveries were made.

When he reached that side of the building, there was only one man in plain clothes. *Yep, this appears to be the best option, but how am I going to get him to move?*

He checked his watch, five minutes remained. He took a deep breath and headed directly for the man posted at the door, hoping that the sheer audacity of what he was about to do would be enough.

Before the guard could even get one word out, Michael dictated orders as quickly as he could.

"Time to rotate positions," he barked. "I'm scheduled to take over here."

"I didn't hear of any rotation plans."

"Of course not," he explained, keeping up his bravado. "The chief just decided a few minutes ago. He felt it would be more effective in keeping everyone alert at their stations by rotating them. You know how staying in one place gets pretty boring."

The guard nodded in agreement buying into his bluff.

"Yeah, that makes sense. Let me call in and check it out."

"No problem." Michael said, acting as though he completely understood the need to verify the change in orders.

As the other man lifted the two-way radio to his mouth, Michael swung as hard as he could. Pain exploded in his fist as he made contact. The man fell to the ground, unconscious with the silenced radio beside him.

"Sorry." He bent over the still figure, scooped up the radio, grabbed his badge and headed through the busy kitchen. No one gave him a second glance as he displayed the badge to establish his right to be there.

There were several different doors toward the back of the kitchen. Michael was not sure which one to open. He figured that one of them led to the hotel dining room. He hoped the other would take him to the ballroom, or at least somewhere close to it.

As he reached a door, a waiter pushed his way through carrying huge empty hors d'oeuvre trays. As the door swung back and forth, the music signaled Michael that he was exactly where he needed to be.

He pushed the door open just a crack. The room was teeming with people. Their costumes created a kaleidoscope of colors reflected everywhere by the mirrored walls. He knew exactly what he was looking for. Slowly, the crowd of people who blocked his view shifted positions. There she was! Her back was toward him, but he knew it was her. The lights caught the beads of her gown giving off the appearance she was shimmering, just like in the images. His heart was pounding like a sludge hammer in his chest.

He looked at his watch. He had two minutes. There was no time to think. He shoved open the door and headed straight for her. Protests erupted from the crowd as they were pushed aside by the un-costumed intruder.

Determined not to be stopped, he moved forward until he reached her. He firmly gripped her arm. She turned, her blue eyes flashed with anger. Her icy stare was met with his expression of concern.

"I'm sorry, Mrs. Paxton, but this time you have to come with me." He turned away and pulled her with him. She tried to speak, but as she did, the band struck a chord of announcement.

Instantly, the crowd around them was caught up in the excitement. No one paid any attention to the two of them. The anticipation intensified as the traditional countdown began.

"Ten!"

Michael held tightly onto the protesting woman as he continued to pull her through the crowd.

"Nine!"

"Michael," she screamed, trying to be heard above the noise.

"Eight!"

"Seven!"

"Michael, please stop!" Her resistance made him even more determined to get her out of the ballroom.

"Six!"

Finally making it out of the main room and into the entryway she stepped back and yanked her arm from his grip. He stopped and turned toward her.

"Five!"

"Michael," she yelled, "I'm Tamara!"

"What?" He looked at her questioningly.

"Four!"

"I'm Tamara," she repeated, yelling louder.

"Your eyes?" he questioned, pointing to her eyes.

"Three!"

Tamara looked confused, and then suddenly she realized what he meant.

"Two!"

"Contacts. Contact lenses!" she screamed.

"One!"

"Oh my God," Michael said, already knowing his mistake could be a fatal one. They both raced back into the ballroom.

Cheers of "Happy New Year" erupted around them. The fabric that held the colorful balloons in place parted, followed by shrieks of delight as the balloons drifted down.

They scanned the ballroom. He spotted Catherine, she was now less than fifty feet away. From the corner of his eye Michael saw security closing in on him, there was no way he was going to let anything stop him. He shoved his way through the frenzied crowd just as the balloons began popping.

Michael had almost reached Catherine's side, but knew he was going to be too late to pull her to safety. There was only one thing he could do. He stepped directly in front of her, shielding her body from what he believed would be the direction of the bullet.

Startled by the physical invasion of an un-costumed young man, the crowd around her stepped back, but Catherine did not move. Michael knew she recognized him. She opened her mouth to speak, but before she could utter a word, a shot rang out, muffled only by the popping of balloons.

Michael's calculations had been correct. He took the bullet full force. Michael fell to the floor, relief overshadowing any pain he should have felt. It was finally over.

Chapter 53

Catherine stood motionless as Detective Costanza made his way to her, his expression softening.

"I'm glad you're all right," the detective said, clearing his throat.

"I'm all right, but…" She looked down at Michael's bloody body, his head cradled in Tamara's lap. Raising her head, she gave the detective a questioning look.

"Don't worry, we've got the shooter," he answered. "We were on him as soon as the shot was fired, but I'm afraid it was not quick enough." Observing the still form on the floor he shook his head. "So this is Michael Peterson?"

Catherine nodded sadly and continued to watch her daughter's unsuccessful attempts to get some type of response from Michael.

"The paramedics are on their way," said a familiar voice from behind her.

Catherine looked up and slowly scanned the crowd of masked faces, stopping on a figure ominously costumed as a dragon.

Instinctively she knew who was behind that hideous mask. "Garrett?"

He hesitated for a moment. "Yes, Mother, it's me."

"I'm so glad you're all right." She moved to him, reaching out to hug him.

His body stiffened at her public display of affection, but she didn't care.

"I am so sorry for all the trouble I've caused you, Mother," he mumbled, making a poor attempt at an apology.

"It's all right, it's all right." Catherine repeated and hugged him tighter.

Detective Costanza moved up protectively beside her. His closeness signaled her that he was uneasy with their exchange.

"Mom…Mom…Mom!"

Catherine turned her head toward the sound of her daughter's distressed pleas. Michael's eyes were open and he was struggling to get to his feet. His stare locked on Garrett, who, still in her embrace, flashed a victorious smile in their direction.

"Michael, stay still," Tamara said, urging him to lay flat. Blood oozed from his shoulder. "Michael, stop," she said louder, but his resolve did not waver. He pulled himself up, wincing as he slowly made his way toward Garrett.

****

Michael recognized that twisted smile. It triggered something deep inside him. He felt one of Elliot's images begin to take over. He knew without a doubt that he was back on the bridge in the silver Mercedes. This was it, there was no turning back.

"Oh my God, I don't believe this," he said. All eyes turned toward him. Michael stood perfectly still willing himself to release his control over what he knew was about to take place.

"Not me. Not now!" He glanced at both the side and rearview mirrors. He recognized the bright red

Lamborghini, the one he had bought his son to bribe him back into college. Checking the mirror again, he caught a glimpse of his son's face twisted into a contorted smile of victory. In that moment he knew there was no point in trying to regain control of his car.

Could it be possible? He knew the answer to his own question. Yes, it was possible. His own son hated him that much. That was Elliot's last thought as the steering wheel crushed the life from him.

"How could you do this to me?" Michael asked with unseeing eyes.

Garrett stepped away from his mother and closer to his accuser.

"Because I hate you, just as you hated me my entire life. Nothing I ever did was good enough for you, was it?" The years of rage continued to spew from him for all to hear. "You're a son of a bitch, and you deserved to die. And I'm glad I did it!"

All eyes in the room shifted from Michael to Garrett. Garrett's face turned as red as a raw piece of meat, his nostrils flaring like a bull about to do battle. He moved in even closer to his target. He threw one well-placed punch, sending Michael to the floor and back into unconsciousness.

****

Catherine watched in shocked silence, cringing as her son's confession sunk in. She turned away no longer being able to look at him. She was repulsed, not only by the kind of person he had become, but also by the sad realization that she had helped create him. Had she loved him too much? Had she saved him once too often? She knew she would never have the answers.

Garrett stood motionless as the handcuffs were

secured around his wrists. Detective Costanza jerked forcefully on Garrett's arm to get him to move.

"Mother, please, you can't possibly believe this guy." He nodded toward where Michael lay on the floor. Catherine looked at Michael and then turned to face her son.

"But I do," she said sadly.

"You believe him? You believe this…this stranger?"

"Yes, I do."

"How could you? This is a trick; he's a con! Surely you can see that!"

"No, this is not a trick, nor is he a con. Not this time. He only wanted to warn me."

She shook her head. She couldn't even begin to explain to her son all that had happened. Silently, she nodded at Detective Costanza, who led Garrett away.

As Garrett was being dragged across the ballroom floor he shouted. "Please, Mother. Please. Help me!"

"I'm sorry, I can't."

"It's not my fault!"

"It was never your fault. I wouldn't let it be." She again turned her back on Garrett and slowly moved toward Tamara, who was still sitting on the ballroom floor with Michael.

The begging suddenly stopped, and again the rage took over. From across the ballroom floor, Garrett screamed obscenities. Then his obscenities suddenly changed back to pleas of help in a desperate attempt to invoke some sense of guilt or motherly duty. This ploy had always worked in the past, but this time Catherine did not come to his aid. She wasn't listening, she wasn't turning. His words no longer held any power over her.

Lauri Broadbent

"I don't need you, you bitch. I never have!" he
screamed as he was led out through the hotel lobby,
down the steps, and placed in a police car that sat ready
at the hotel entrance.

Shortly after the police car departed, an ambulance
arrived and two attendants swiftly secured Michael's
unconscious body onto a gurney. Gently, they moved
him out and into the waiting ambulance, which left with
sirens screaming.

As the crowd dissipated, many expressed their
sympathies to Catherine and quickly took the
opportunity to leave. Not long after, having had their
fill, the curious hangers-on also left. Alone in the empty
ballroom, mother and daughter looked at each other,
Catherine was emotionally exhausted and saddened by
the turn of events. She could see that her daughter was
visibly shaken by all that had transpired and couldn't
blame her; she was shaken too. She felt like a pawn in a
game in which she had no idea she was playing.

"Tamara," she said softly, "it will be all right." She
took her daughter into her arms and held her tightly.
Tamara's body began to shake with sobs. "Shhhh…we
will be okay."

"I feel so guilty, I should have listened to him, but
it was all so…so weird."

"I know, I know, we both were so quick to judge
and now someone who only wanted my safety may pay
the price with his life."

"And what about Garrett?" Tamara choked out his
name. "I can't believe he did what he did…how could
he? I knew he hated Dad, but this?' Tamara began to
cry again.

"Sweetheart." Catherine firmly pushed Tamara

240

back, though still holding on tightly to her forearms. She needed to look directly into her daughter's pain-filled face and make sure Tamara listened to every word she was about to say. "You have no part in how your brother made his choices. Garrett has some serious problems. He's had them for years."

Catherine took a deep breath and let it out. "I guess I didn't want to see them. I always believed if I loved him enough everything would eventually turn out okay, but as we now know, it didn't. I feel I am partly responsible for you losing your father, but I don't want you to live your life wrapped in anger because of the mistakes your father and I made. That's exactly what Garrett did."

Tamara started to disagree with her but was silenced by the shake of her mother's head. "Maybe if I had done something sooner, none of this would have happened." Her voice was filled with sadness.

Looking directly into eyes that matched her own, Catherine reached out and tucked up a piece of Tamara's blonde hair that had escaped from beneath her beaded cap.

"You know, I really do like the color of your eyes," she teased, trying to lighten the serious look on her daughter's face.

"Thanks, Mom. I knew you would." She hugged her mother.

"I'm ready to go, are you?" Catherine asked.

"Yes, I am *so* ready."

They turned and walked toward the front entrance.

Catherine felt the quiet strength of Thomas Scottford well up inside of her. She knew he would be proud of them.

241

They had the strength to get through this and they would get through this together.

Chapter 54

Dr. Whitney had him do one more arm rotation. "Well, Michael, it looks like that shoulder of yours has healed quite nicely," he said as he patted Michael's shoulder. "Not that it's any of my business, but have you attempted to speak to any of the Paxtons since all this happened?"

"No, I'm not sure it's the right thing to do."

Dr. Whitney nodded his head. "I can understand how you could feel that way, almost as if it was an invasion of their privacy."

"You have to admit, Dr. Whitney, it's a pretty strange way to meet people." He smiled at the older man. The doctor laughed at Michael's observation.

"Well, since we're speaking of strange"—a smile tugged at the corners of his mouth—"Miss Paxton has called and inquired about you several times."

"She has?" He tried to hide the rush of pleasure he felt.

"Yes, she has. There was something she wanted you to know but didn't want to approach you herself. Guess she didn't want to intrude in your life, either."

"What did she want me to know?"

"It was something about a black metal box."

"What about the metal box?" Michael asked excitedly.

"She wanted you to know that the metal box she

found in her father's desk drawer held a letter of confirmation regarding the attempt on Catherine's life. All the information was right there."

"I figured there had to be some sort of connection."

"Seems so," the doctor agreed. "I guess in the end, father and son were not as different as they thought they were."

Michael nodded. He was glad the whole thing was over. He finally felt in control of his own destiny and no longer had the urge to protect anyone else.

The images had slowly subsided over the last couple of months, replaced by pleasant dreams of a beautiful blonde with sparkling green eyes.

"Well, that about does it. You can get dressed now. I will want to see you in about a month. Oh, and Michael?" The doctor cleared his throat. "I want you to know…you did the right thing."

He smiled at the doctor, knowing this was as close to an apology as he was ever going to get. Having Dr. Whitney's approval was important. He hadn't realized how important it was until the doctor had actually said it.

"Thank you."

The doctor continued. "And it might interest you to know, not only did the Paxtons donate all the proceeds from their ball to my research, but through their corporation I have also received offers from all over the world to fund the continuation of this project."

"Congratulations, that's great." Michael was pleased that breaking his word had actually turned out to be beneficial to them both.

Stepping down from the table, Michael extended his hand, "Thanks again, Dr. Whitney."

"Thank you, Michael," the doctor said tightly shaking the younger man's hand. "Call if you need anything."

"I will." Michael replied as the doctor exited the room.

After dressing, Michael left the office and walked a short distance in the warm sunshine to where he had parked his car. Climbing in, he decided there was one more stop he needed to make.

****

Thirty minutes later, as he approached the glass enclosure, the security guard turned in his direction.

"May I help you, sir?"

"I would like to see Miss Paxton."

"Is she expecting you?"

Michael paused for a moment. "Yes, I think she is."

A word from the author...

I am published in *Chicken Soup for the Parent's Soul* and have written pieces for the former Nevada newsletter, the *Clark County Chronicles*.